THE
QUARTERLY

EDITED BY

GORDON LISH

The question probably is—
how come are we
doing a number
with work by only women in it?

Okay, good question.

As for Harris and Nace,
forget it.

THE Q WANTS TO CITE THE NAME OF A PHYSICIAN,
HIMSELF A WRITER,
WHO HAS MINISTERED, IS MINISTERING,
TO CERTAIN WRITERS WHO HAVE PUBLISHED,
ARE PUBLISHING,
IN THESE PAGES.
HIS NAME IS MARC SIEGEL.
THANK YOU, THANK YOU,
AND THANK GOD FOR YOU,
DR. SIEGEL.

THE
QUARTERLY

18 / SUMMER 1991

VINTAGE BOOKS

A DIVISION OF RANDOM HOUSE, INC.

NEW YORK

COPYRIGHT © 1991 BY THE QUARTERLY
ALL RIGHTS RESERVED UNDER INTERNATIONAL AND PAN-AMERICAN
COPYRIGHT CONVENTIONS. PUBLISHED IN THE UNITED STATES BY VINTAGE BOOKS,
A DIVISION OF RANDOM HOUSE, INC., NEW YORK, AND SIMULTANEOUSLY IN
CANADA BY RANDOM HOUSE OF CANADA LIMITED, TORONTO.

THE QUARTERLY (ISSN: 0893-3103) IS EDITED BY GORDON LISH
AND IS PUBLISHED MARCH, JUNE, SEPTEMBER, AND DECEMBER AT
201 EAST 50TH STREET, NEW YORK, NY 10022. SUBSCRIPTIONS—
FOUR ISSUES AT $40 US, $54 CANADIAN, $46 US OVERSEAS—AND ADDRESS
CHANGES SHOULD BE SENT TO THE ATTENTION OF SUBSCRIPTION OFFICE,
28TH FLOOR. ORDERS RECEIVED BY JANUARY 31 START WITH MARCH NUMBER;
BY APRIL 30, JUNE NUMBER; BY JULY 31, SEPTEMBER NUMBER; BY OCTOBER 31,
DECEMBER NUMBER. SEE LAST PAGE FOR PURCHASE OF BACK NUMBERS.

MANAGEMENT BY ELLEN F. TORRON
EDITORIAL ASSISTANCE BY RICK WHITAKER

THE QUARTERLY WELCOMES THE OPPORTUNITY TO READ WORK OF EVERY
CHARACTER, AND IS ESPECIALLY CONCERNED TO KEEP ITSELF AN OPEN FORUM.
MANUSCRIPTS MUST BE ACCOMPANIED BY THE CUSTOMARY RETURN MATERIALS,
AND SHOULD BE ADDRESSED TO THE EDITOR. THE QUARTERLY MAKES THE UTMOST
EFFORT TO OFFER ITS RESPONSE TO MANUSCRIPTS NO LATER THAN ONE WEEK
SUBSEQUENT TO RECEIPT. OPINIONS EXPRESSED HEREIN ARE NOT NECESSARILY
THOSE OF THE EDITOR OR OF THE PUBLISHER.

ISBN: 0-679-73495-3

DESIGN BY ANDREW ROBERTS
INSTALLATION BY DENISE STEWART

YES, YES, THE TERESA LEONE WHOSE FICTION APPEARS IN Q18 BELONGS TO
THE SAME LEONE FAMILY THAT GAVE EXPRESSION TO DOM AND DAN LEONE.
NOT THAT THE Q IS STRUGGLING TO DEMONSTRATE ANY PARTICULAR AFFECTION
FOR THE LEONES. IT IS JUST FAMILIES THAT WE LIKE, SHOULD YOU BE
CONCERNED TO HAVE OUR EXPLANATION. WHICH RAISES THE MATTER OF
YUNG LUNG, THIS ISSUE NEPOTISTICALLY—AND THIS LOWERS THE MATTER—
YING LING. FINALLY, SUBSCRIBERS AND CONTRIBUTORS WILL PLEASE NOTE
THAT PUNISHING STEPS ARE BEING TAKEN TO SPEED UP THE DELIVERY
OF COPIES AND THE DELIVERY OF PAYMENT. IT MIGHT HELP FOR YOU
TO BEAR IN MIND THAT, TREMENDOUS AS WE THINK WE ARE, WE ARE LITTLE,
LITTLE, LITTLE, WITH A STAFF THAT IS TEENSY-TINY BUT WITH AN INTAKE
OF MAIL THAT IS GREATER THAN NEW ZEALAND'S. AND NOW POSITIVELY FINALLY,
RICK BASS GOT HIMSELF AN NEA, WHICH HAPPY NEWS YOU WOULD
HAVE HEARD FROM US IN Q17—IF WE HAD.

MANUFACTURED IN THE UNITED STATES OF AMERICA

THE QUARTERLY

FIRST, HARRIS

A NACE PAGE   2

PATRICIA LEAR / *Ironman*   3

CHRISTINE SCHUTT /
  Three Fictions   13

ELIZABETH EVANS / *Blood and Gore*   36

DIANE HOPKINS /
  The Nipple of the Queen   40

TERESA LEONE / *Sandwich*   50

SARAH CHACE / *The Acts*   52

DIANE DESANDERS /
  A Piece of the Angel   56

DAWN RAFFEL / *Four Fictions*   67

LILY TUCK / *Every Time I Have a Cup
  of This Tea, I Will Think of Africa*   76

LISA WOHL / *Two Fictions*   90

DIANE WILLIAMS / *Fifteen Fictions*   93

LYNN GROSSMAN / *Raising Mom*   109

EILEEN HENNESSY / *The Translator*   112

VICTORIA REDEL /
  Ruby, Darwin, Eurydice   154

KATHRYN THOMPSON / *PV=nRT*   157

C. C. LANDSMAN /
  My Mother Dressing   160

THE QUARTERLY

CECILE GODING /
   Mr. and Mrs. from Missouri   *164*

ELEANOR ALPER /
   We Started with Childcraft   *170*

KATHERINE ARNOLDI /
   Canton, Ohio: 1956   *172*

ANOTHER NACE PAGE   *174*

SUSAN RAWLINS   *175*

SUZANNE PAOLA   *179*

MICHELLE RHEA   *181*

MARJORIE MILLIGAN   *182*

KIM BRIDGFORD   *183*

VICTORIA REDEL   *190*

LYNNE H. DECOURCY   *192*

ANSIE BAIRD   *193*

MARY LEADER   *194*

JOAN KINCAID   *199*

SARAH RANDOLPH   *201*

CAROL LEE   *203*

GAIL WRONSKY   *205*

ONE MORE NACE PACE   *206*

PAULETTE JILES *to Q*   *207*

HEATHER KEE *to Q*   *209*

LILLIAN STUART *to Q*   *216*

THE QUARTERLY

PAULETTE JILES *to* Q   220
PATRICIA MARX *to* Q   222
ENID CRACKEL *to* Q   223
ISABELLA BANNERMAN *to* Q   224
ANNA KAINEN *to* Q   228
JANE MARTIN *to* Q   232
YING LING *to* Q   233
PAULETTE JILES *to* Q   238
ROBIN CHMELAR *to* Q   245
ENID CRACKEL *to* Q   246
THE LAST NACE PAGE   247

First, Harris

Those of us who can imagine no fate more glamorous than being immortalized as the patron saint of the First Amendment greeted Rushdie's change of heart with reserve, a polite disappointment that masked our outrage at his ungrateful forfeiture of a golden opportunity for martyrdom. Reporters shied away from the word "recantation," but that indeed was what it was, a complete and uncompromising retraction reminiscent in its absurdity of the frantic back-pedalling of Chaucer and Boccaccio—an action that, in a secular culture like our own, seemed at once quaintly obsolete and staggeringly implausible. Like a victim of torture who concedes everything after he feels the first jolts of electricity surging through his genitals, Rushdie came clean, breaking down and pleading guilty, his face screwed up into an anxiously conciliatory grin in order to allay the savagery of those who placed such a high price on his pelt. But of course it is cruel to demand heroism from anyone. Safely ensconced behind our desks, we exploited Rushdie for more than two years as a beast of burden for the Western intellectual conscience before he finally buckled under the weight of the dangerous life of international intrigue we experienced vicariously through him. It is no wonder, then, that, given the way in which he ultimately balked at our expectations, we are full of righteous indignation at his uncooperative insistence on being a man rather than a messiah. Instead of allowing us to bury him in our ideals and eulogize his remains in the name of free speech, he shattered the solemn silence of our mourning by battering thunderously on the lid of the coffin in which we had so generously interred him. My hopes dashed, I find myself wanting to preserve an uncanny moment in literary history, one that clashes dramatically with the image of the Western writer I know so well: that of the harmless intellectual battening on princely honoraria or chewing the cud at writers' workshops and book parties in New York. In Rushdie's recantation, we see our culture as we have never seen it before: frightened, on the run, begging for mercy, grovelling on its knees, and acceding to the demands of extortionists, while those of us immunized, by virtue of our anonymity, against the threat of Islam follow what has become almost a spectator sport, safe and snug with our principles in the peanut gallery.

—D H

THE

QUARTERLY

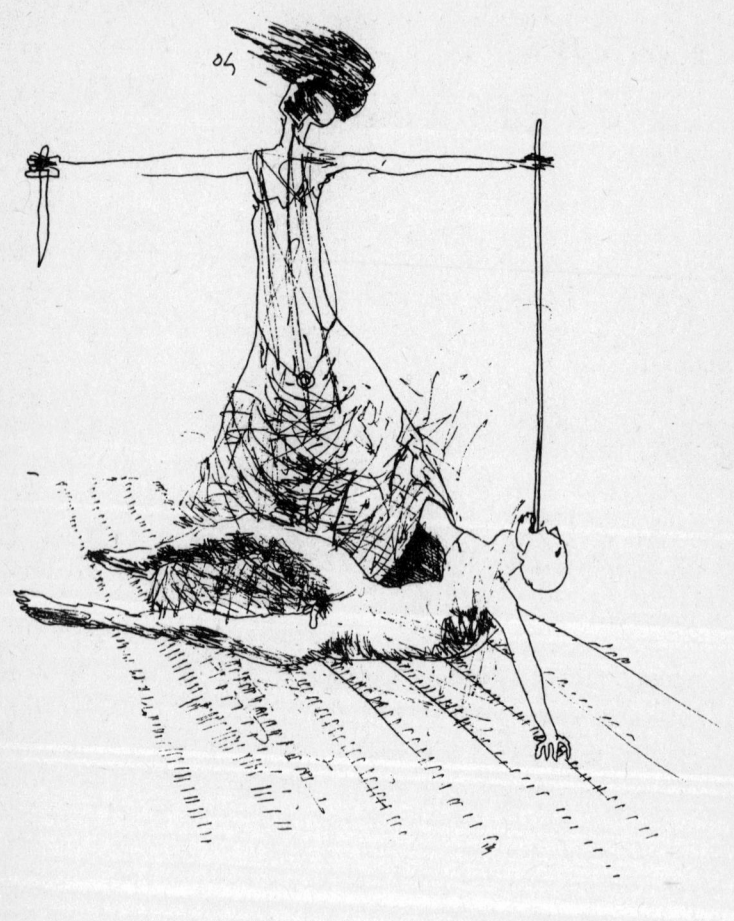

slowing that woman down

PATRICIA LEAR

Ironman

I am recently living at Lloyd's with Lloyd and his dog, Blackie. Lloyd is my young lover, of an Asian background, and Blackie is a decent dog somebody else probably used to own. With the windows thrown wide and the desert stars outside showing through punch holes in the night sky, Blackie sleeps curled around on herself with Lloyd and me in the king-sized water bed, and she bobs there down at the foot of the bed on a collection of Indian blankets we keep ready in case of cold.

How it usually goes in the early mornings is Lloyd kicking the old comforter off the bed, where it parachutes down across the room, it's so old, with the goosedown squashed flat, and then us getting our running clothes on and lacing up our high-tech, state-of-the-art, gel-cushioned training shoes, and slapping out the side screen porch door, with Blackie snaking out through the first crack of unfettered sunlight either of us makes in the door, and her firing off like a rifle shot chasing through the weeds.

Lloyd and I follow. We trot gently up to the path high in the hills to warm up, shaking out our arms and legs as we go along, winding and doing hairpin crookbacks and nice banked turns up close by on hard-packed clay. When the path straightens out and we get going and ease into our real run, one and then the other one of us has to fight off Blackie for the lead, which has some danger in it because Blackie has a problem with jumping and nipping with her tiny front teeth.

Talk about horizons. At the break of dawn, when the sun rollers color up over the running hills in clear soft shapes, we are looking at the whole world from up there on our early-morning runs, running with our feet low, kicking along the ground, and thinking only about our breathing rhythms or which way we might want to go next. In this way, we pack in anywhere from a twelve- to twenty-miler, six solid days a week.

Okay, I got to say it now, something you don't need to know if you are a woman like me, or will want to hear about if you are a man like my husband, Moss, is, but young guys are nice, and to me, a better thing than living with an old man your own age. Things crash around and there are wild tricks. There is an off-balance quality to our life—Lloyd's and Blackie's and mine. None of us matches. In other ways of course, we do, we do, we really do.

Okay. We listen to a rock station on the radio in Lloyd's old piece of shit of a car, and I believe in, and like, most of the songs. When we make love, Lloyd and I, we use our whole flat open hands over our whole flat open bodies. We use our mouths. We even roll Blackie, old weird Blackie, over on her back and kiss her stomach and take deep sniffs of her neck fur. We scoot Blackie over to give us some room and I do things like crawl between Lloyd's legs and hang tail-to-the-wind off his side. We aren't afraid to try things is what I mean. Then we sleep, then we run, then we eat, and that's about it; that's our little life.

Well, I say our life makes easily as much sense as my husband Moss's ever did, or even what I can figure out from watching other people in their lives.

Moss would stuff his fingers in his ears if he heard me talking about my life now, that it could be any better than his and my little piddling jaunts to the Workout World.

I am now a triathlete, among about one other thing, and when my mom sees the senior female bodybuilders on weekend TV (they are everywhere now), she calls me up and she says, "What in the world, Crystal, just what in the world? Those silly women, you don't want to look like those women, do you, Crystal?"

Well, yes, surprise! surprise! I think I do. I am beginning to like more and more what I see when I see those women, and when I tell my mom this, she has been known to hang up on me. What she needs to understand is that her daughter's eye for beauty is undergoing a transformation.

What I have been working on these past couple of years is really getting a grip on things. It has been important to be pushing to the edge of things. There was a point at the tail end of the being-together part of our marriage, Moss's and mine, where my life measured about an inch, registered a zero on the Richter scale. It was all I could do just to get out of bed in the mornings, sometimes just so I could get back in it for the rest of the day until it was time to get back out again. I would smoke cigarettes! and drink grapefruit juice, and try to sleep dressed in spandex and leggings from the one thing I did. Moss would be saying, his wife pinioned to the bed with an ache in her soul, he would say, "Well, that's tough, babe." Then Moss would have to go on out to earn us a living, smelling of his Christmas-present after-shave, he would go out into the world and drive to his office, or drive to a meeting, or he would pull on some pineapple-patterned golf pants and throw his clubs in the back of the car to earn us a living doing business golf on the golf course. So here's what I did.

I did the Ironman.

Life has ways of being hard for all of us. It has been hard on Lloyd, with his pearly skin and funny English, and even on Blackie, who has tar-colored bare skin patches on her where her fur will not grow anymore. She is probably an older dog—I don't know how many years exactly—but even if she is a young dog, she has clearly had a hard life. More than anything, I would kind of like to know exactly what happened to Blackie, so I could quit thinking of things, envisioning things—sadistic tortures, cruel abandonments, hit-and-run car accidents, and so I could make all the needed exceptions for her bad habits, such as her endless barking, and give her all the necessary time to come around to a deeper trust. What I do for Blackie is, I let her, as I said, sleep with Lloyd and me, and I give her long runs over the mountains and spend extra money on some scientific dog food the vet says is the best.

But as you know, there is always going to be something.

This is real life, not heaven. You don't really just do the Ironman and find yourself a young boyfriend and have that be it, have it be the last thing, have the hard times be all nice and neat and behind you. With life, like ocean swimming, there's waves and undercurrents and good days and bad days and, as you know, you never know.

The facts are that, for a while now, I won't be going out with Lloyd and Blackie on our early-morning runs. The facts are that, for a while now, there won't be any strapping on the little ankle weights and doing distance, any intervals or any fartlek, no down on the beach running backward and running forward, no visits with the foot doctor, no signing up for races, no scrambling up the hills and scrambling back down the hills, kicking up storms of dust with rocks and cinders mixed in. The facts are that Lloyd'll be leaving me back in the bed while he and Blackie slap out the screen door, just the two of them, sort of like fuckhead Moss used to do when Moss would be going off someplace or throwing his golf clubs into the back of the car. You see, what happened was that eight days, seven hours, and twenty-four minutes ago, while doing my hillwork, I slid off a hill. Lloyd was with me. Blackie had chased off barking like the stupid-dog-dumb-fuck she can at times be. The rest, however you imagine the rest, is the way it was.

Eileen is the woman I found in the yellow pages after I saw what I was going to be doing was just lying out here on my back in the chaise longue or the canvas butterfly chair under the firecracker tree getting out of the way of myself. I mean, she is the one I have my phone consultations with, or sessions with, or whatever you want to call them. She was the one on the other end of the Help Hotline the first time I called. Her full name is Eileen-something-something-Jewish-plus-some-degree, and one of the things I've been discussing with Eileen is how I think I don't do at all well anymore just lying places.

To which Eileen says, "Crystal, you healed your life once. You can do it again."

To which I say to Eileen, "Eileen, it's too hard. I can't go through all that saving of myself again."

Back with Moss—it was in a movie theater with my leg pulled over Moss's leg, never touching the popcorn once, not one single kernel, never seeing the movie either, that I started thinking. The lights went down, and by the time the trailers were over, I was loose from the world and off in my head picking at my life's scabs, just fingernailing them up and getting the blood to flow and looking at what it was that was driving me so crazy. The things I found would just make me think love more, think life more, while Moss was sitting there watching the movie and reaching his hand into my jeans to walk his fingers around in there. And his hand was not romance, either. I do not know what it was, but it was not romance. And you know what? I still cannot figure out what to do about it either—you know, that it wasn't.

We make plans in the mornings. Being newly confined as I am, I have come to notice what I never really looked at and noticed before. Such as Lloyd himself.

Eileen says about him, when I bring it up with her in our phone sessions with what she calls sheer wonderment in my voice, Eileen says, "Well, Crystal, look who's there with him. Think about that and we will talk some more tomorrow."

Mornings go like this now. Us all awake. Blackie zinging through all the rooms of the house. Lloyd lacing up his running shoes, keeping Blackie at bay with an elbow; Lloyd's ears girlish, showing through splits in his hair. Together, dog and man trot out to the path, and I watch them as far as I can see them go, me wrapped in an Indian blanket, from my place in the upstairs bed.

I get in the tub pretty much on schedule—just like I had a schedule. Then Blackie shows up first to lap water out of the toilet. Lloyd comes in next, glistening and slick and wiping his brow off with his wadded shirt, then dropping his clothes to pool on the floor, kicking the pile over to soak up where I have sloshed water over the sides of the tub. I look at his ankles, how hard things inside his ankles move as Lloyd shifts his weight, barefooted and hunched over while brushing his teeth, or even while taking long, foot-long pulls back through his hair with my wide-tooth wooden comb before he disappears down the hall to the shower.

Since it has quit raining—at least in the mottled shade of the firecracker tree—I sit grasshopper-positioned in the canvas butterfly chair, doing what they tell me to do. I am fighting sliding into that crevice between how things are and how I want them to be, and mentally am trying to make up a list of things to discuss with Eileen when it is our scheduled time to talk. I keep the cordless lying out here next to me on the bricks, and after a while I kind of, how you do, sit blurred and unfocused . . . I bog down.

Maybe this is what depression is.

Blackie goes nuts with barking, which means nothing to me, means squirrel or garbageman or leaf—such is Blackie—but I feel the tickling of something brushing my forehead. Could be anything, but there is also breathing as well, so I focus my eyes and see my husband Moss's face above me.

"Thought I'd make a courtesy call in person on the shut-in," Moss says (over Blackie's barking like a maniac), while he is pulling himself up straight and holding, like bowling pins, two glass bottles of Coke swinging loose in his free hand, his fingers just lightly pinching their frosty necks.

Moss drops down on the redwood bench next to my butterfly chair and shoves all my magazines off onto the bricks of the patio. "Business trip," he says, as he puts one hand under his chin and unbunches the fingers to tap on his cheekbone. "Ramada Inn," he says.

On my blaster is playing one of those teenage songs about

smoking joints and rolling around on top of women, and Blackie is still up on her feet, still suspicious and giving out little half barks through her lips.

"What did I ever do to you, Crystal?" Moss says, looking to me like he just got out of a shower, with the ends of his hair spiky with something wet. Then he stands up, setting a take-out bag on the end of the bench, and turns and goes up the stairs to the kitchen.

I yell after him, "Hey! I don't eat this stuff! Leave anything you brought for me right in the bag, Moss."

Moss waves me off, kind of fluttering a hand behind him as he peels off his suit jacket and twirls it around his shoulders in a way I never saw him do before. His white shirt sticks to a spot in the middle of his back.

Next, I see Moss up there violating the serenity of Lloyd's hand-rubbed-by-my-hands white pine kitchen, slamming drawers and getting glasses and cracking ice-cube trays and pulling sheets of paper towel off a roll next to the sink. "We got to talk, babe," Moss says, a paper towel easing through the air to settle itself undersea-like on the floor, Moss leaning into the door jamb with just his upper body, still busy messing with something in front of him on the counter. I am getting my arms and legs arranged and mentally negotiating my mind around my pain, and then standing myself up smack into the center of the pain so I can hobble up the stairs, and wedge past Moss, saying "Bathroom" to him, and then I go on upstairs to put in a call to Eileen on the cordless I carry up there with me—I say, "Get Eileen," to whoever's taking calls on the Hotline, all the time trying to occupy myself with envisioning Eileen's face.

I envision Eileen completely different every time.

I lie down on the water bed to wait for her return call; sometimes it takes a couple of minutes and sometimes, if she is away, sometimes it takes a very long time. I do a few of my leg raises and pelvic tilts for my back, scared to tie up the line with calling Lloyd where he works selling sleeping bags and mountain-trek adventure supplies, though I would like to do just that, call Lloyd and call Eileen both. Blackie is on me like a flash, tussling around and tidal-waving the bed—I fend her off with my foot.

Eileen says, when she calls back, "Oh, that's wonderful, Crystal. It's a circus, it's a circus! What an opportunity!" then Blackie jumps on me again and Moss comes to the bottom of the stairs and says my name. I take two sticks of gum from the bedside table and carefully unwrap them and accordion them up neatly before I put them in my mouth. I hobble back down the stairs and back past Moss and go outside, where I lower myself into the chaise, keeping my arms elbow-locked as long as I can and lowering myself by taking the weight as much as possible with my shoulders.

I see Moss is walking back down the steps carrying a tray, and his big white shirt is inflating out from his suit pants in places where the wind gets in.

"You've done it now, Crystal," he says. "Tell me, what all *have* you done to yourself, Crystal?"

He wolfs his piled-up hot dog, tearing off small pieces for Blackie and throwing them overhanded to the farthest corner of the patio, and then he eats the hot dog he expected I would eat, plus all of the french fries, too.

The sun in the sky begins to fade, as it does at that time of day, and Moss says to me, "I think it's kind of funny. I'm kind of impressed with you actually, Crystal," he says.

Then he says to me, as I watch him stand up and do a final little practice swing like he had a golf club in his hand, "You know, Crystal, this whole thing should bother me. I don't know why it doesn't bother me—because it should. But it doesn't."

We can almost see the roof of the Ramada from here, from where Lloyd and Blackie and I have got ourselves in our water bed at all of 10 o'clock of a night. We are sitting in the dark without the TV on, or even our eerie lava light, just a little desert moon to flesh out our outlines.

Lloyd is buck-naked and yellowish, leaning up against some feather pillows he has jammed up hard against the headboard, and there are two hanks of his hair sliding down over his shoulders and glowing softly, just like I want them to be—he's out of a fantasy, man, like satin sheets look spilling off beds in Moss's *Penthouse* magazines; none of us ever actually has had satin sheets to spill, but I've had Lloyd. I am in my underpants, and Lloyd has pulled me up against him by wrapping one arm around my rib cage and heaving me up so I am laid against him on a slant, like I was laid out in the chaise longue all day long out back of the house, healing. Lloyd sticks one hand between my legs and looks out at the moon.

Blackie is standing up on all fours, walking around the bed and stopping to bark in obnoxious little rapid-fire-bursts-of-dog-bark out through the window—I guess at the lights of the Ramada, where Moss is probably in the lounge by now, seated at a little square table with a Rob Roy, watching the show they put on there on Thursday nights. There is a girl singer.

Just knowing Moss is down there makes me uneasy. I imagine Moss floating up here and wreathing around us, like the smoky incense in the clay holder shaped like a tepee we picked up down in Santa Fe I've got going across the room, burning on Lloyd's old scratched-up bureau.

I tell Lloyd what's on my mind and he says, oh, hell, he doesn't care about Moss. Moss doesn't care about us. Moss isn't any big thing.

   Next Moss has taken to, on a regular basis, crunching up our road with rolls and coffee, in his business attire, after Lloyd is off to the mountain store, or Moss will come after a breakfast meeting at the Ramada, or after a lunch function, or in the late afternoons with some champagne, or some kind of wine, and plastic cups. He brought a medium-sized ice sculpture day before yesterday. Also some little salmon mousse canapes with capers on top from the same cocktail reception as the ice sculpture. Also, there have been hard little sweet rolls with icing that Lloyd and I have been eating at night in bed that came from a breakfast buffet.

Eileen said many things during our last phone consultation, while all this going back and forth was winding up, and with me lying out back of Lloyd's in the firecracker shade with the cordless, huddled with a towel over my head, trying to find a comfortable position—and Moss upstairs packing up my things. I had said to Eileen, "What about the human dignity of love, Eileen?" but this one thing she never exactly answered, meaning—what about it, for me to figure it out.

Back home with Moss, while resting in the upstairs bed, when my mom called up, I put it to her, you know, the same old thing—after we had worked through all the local newsy news. I said to her, "What about the human dignity of love? What about love?" and my mom said, "What in the world, Crystal? Just what in the world? What is this thing you are trying to say?" **Q**

CHRISTINE SCHUTT

You Drive

She brought him what she had promised, and they did it on the top floor of the car park in his car, looking down onto the black, flat roofs of buildings, and she said, or she thought she said, "I like your skin," when what she really liked was the color of her father's skin, the mottled white of his arms, and the clay color at the roots of the hairs along his arms. Long hair along his arms bleached from sun and water. Sun off the lake, and all that time he spent in water; summer to summer abrading the wild, dry hair on his head, turning the ends of his hair, which was also red, and deeply so, quite white. "You look healthy," she said to her father, and he did, in high color, but the skin on his face seemed coarse to her. Not boy's skin, her father's, not glossy, close-grained skin, but pitted and stubbled under all that color, rashed along his jaw and neck, her father's skin: rough. She touched him, and it was rough skin, his cheek. "Just testing," she said, and smiled at her father. "Shaving," she said. "I used to watch Mother's guys at it."

Her father said, "My youngest daughter still," then he took hold of her hand and kissed it. He was quiet. Holding her hand against his leg and looking out at a roof where a fat woman waited on her dog, her father was quiet. "What a dirty place this is," he said. "That dog is ashamed of himself."

"Look at my hands," she said. "I've seen lots of things," she said, changing the sheets of incontinent patients on rounds made twice a night. All of them up, anyway, these old howlers. Mean and balked and full of worry, the naked woman with her pocket book on her way to the baby, the farmer at the window. He thinks the nurse's station is a bar. "Where the fuck," the farmer says over and over. "You should know this about me," she said to her father. "I can take care of myself."

"So tell me what you have seen," her father said, and she told him about her mother and the guy with the criminal haircut. "Can you imagine?" she asked her father. The two of them, inviting her in after, turning the pillows over and over and fanning at their chests by lifting up the sheet. And there was more, she said, a lot more, but it was her father's turn. "You promised," she said. "The wife."

"The wife," he said.

The wife has see-through skin and grainy eyelids bruised by nature. When she wakes, there's all this sand between her lashes. Daughters, too. Brown and knobby daughters, dozens of them, scotch-taping bangs and walking through the house in their underwear.

She told her father a girl had kissed her once, and not a girl really, but a woman, a teacher, a small, dark, trembly woman who followed all the games at school, running herself breathless up and down the playing field.

"How did it feel?" her father asked, "to kiss a woman?"

"I don't remember," she said. "The woman turned teacherly and took me by the shoulders."

"You are such a show-off," T said. "You are vain. You are braggy."

She told her father about these girls she knew who were in love with one another. They let her watch them kiss at the lake after swimming. Their kissing was not so dry or hard-seeming as the kissing she remembered with her teacher. The blonde abundance of the girl-girl curled outside the suit. So much smoke in the car, she did not know if she imagined the square and heavy ends of her father's fingers, or if she saw or had hold of his fingers. The whorled, dead-white ends of his fingers, tips weighted as surely as a line, deep fishing, plummet of fat in the black-green water—what was that thing he said he caught? Lifted out of the water and beating against her, the fish curling and uncurling in the heat of her hand.

"Tell me about your boyfriends," her father said. Her father said, "Who else besides the character who gets you this stuff?"

"Just the character," she said, and she called the character T because she didn't want to give him a name. A name could get them all in trouble. "T is just a hairless boy—doesn't need to shave," she said. Same age, but not her size. Smaller, prettier—a lean girl's face, sharp angles, good bones. The hammocked skin underneath his eyes fluttered when he kissed. "I look," she said.

Her father kissed her, his dry lips slack against her own and soft. Gentle enough, this time; she could have looked, but she was shy. Ready to move in what ways he moved, toward her or away, a lot depending on the things she brought him. That's what she thought at least, that's what she told him, but her father said, "No, no, no."

Her father said, "My problem is, I'm tired."

Another boy, another car, she used to let him feel her up just so long as she could sleep. "The night shift," she said to her father, "is such a bitch. You're always tired. I can't talk," she said, and she kissed her father. She opened her mouth to him and snuck her hand inside his coat and felt the warm, damp of his shirt, the hard back and heat of her father. Here was no girl-boy, but heavy muscle and bone, soft, wide shoulders, and something like breasts. She liked to push against and rub her face between her father's breasts. She rubbed her face in him: lemons and gin and earth and smoke. His springy hair in her teeth, everywhere springy, and fragrant and wet and tasting of nails. Yes, the metals in my mouth, she said, are singing.

She told T she couldn't remember where she had parked her car.

That was why she was late, she told T. This was another time she couldn't remember. They had driven around and around, she and her father, looking for the street. Honest, she said, but T didn't believe her, and he put his hand in under her skirt to prove it.

T said, "You are so fucking easy to get at," which she supposed was true, the way she dressed, the way she velcroed shut, ready to unravel for a boy—any boy, or that was what T said. "I can see through your dress," T said. "I know what you've been doing."

Under the watchful eye of a man whose name she did not now remember, she took off her skinny bra. He only wanted to look, the man said, and touch her, just a little.
You'd like my mother, she said to the man. You should see my mother.

"Should I be ashamed?" she asked her father. The lady and her dog were gone; only skin-colored fence for a guardrail.
"Of what?" he asked.
Third party to things, watching, scattering other women's charms like seed and clucking in a backward shuffle was how she saw herself, asking, "Do you like that woman? Did you see her breasts?"
Her father said, "I like your breasts."

Full, snub-nosed breasts, nipples tightened in the cold the size of quarters, she liked these breasts, too, and girls with boy-chests and ribs showing through, which wasn't the way she was made or maybe it was, she wasn't sure—even though she looked when she was being touched. She knew these feelings. The damp press and hurtful weight of a man's head against her collar—beard, no beard—she had known this.

"Everyone else," she told her father, "seems to have what I want."

Her father said, "My daughters are the same." Spoiled girls, using Daddy's credit cards to clean beneath their nails, asking can we, why don't we, we should. Her father said, "I don't think of you that way," and he pressed the heel of his hand against her hip as he might to push away, to push off, hard body arched, moving stiffly in the cold waters just off the rocks.

The summer houses shut up for the winter. November, midday, and the black lake flat against the yellow shore. "We could go there," her father said, but they stayed put, in his car, and used the things she brought.

T said, "Even your mother wants it," and she was surprised.

T said, "Oh, come on, everything you fucking do on that nightshift fucking job is crooked."

"What do you do," she asked her father, "when you are not with me?"

He said, "You don't really want to know," and he drove her to an unfinished place and pointed. "I have something to do with that." She saw a building, girders, cloths, nets, menacing vacancies. Her father pointed. "Nobody home," he said, "but that's not my job." Rocking the car easy over the scrubboard road, raising dust, her father said, "We'll never get this thing finished."

Dust settling on the canvased shapes, dumpsters and cinderblock, the whole wild modern array of it—amazing.

"Amazing," she said to her father, looking out the window and back at him: the whiteness of his collar against the blaze of neck, the creases darkened, almost black. At his throat, a tie knotted tight as a knuckle.

Maybe he draws the buildings; maybe he warehouses nails and joints, figure-eight pieces, metal supports. Who knows? The way her father palmed the wheel of his fat car, he might very well be a crook with a crook's car, much like an office, plush and neutral, her father's make, coppery glitter and paneling that might or might not be real wood. Black and gold buttons for everything; the music on the radio—never clearer. Only decide, decide, please. You pick, no you, was the way she was with her father, first word always yes to everything he asked about. Yes, I did. Yes, I will.

Yes when he surprised her, coming up almost to her house and pointing to a shut eye. "Do you believe my wife did this?" he asked, the good eye blinking and teary and strained. "Can you come out with me for just a while?" Yes.

Yes, Dad: the name warmed her every time she used it to his face so that she rarely used this name—or any other to his face. Instead, she signaled him. She gave directions in the way she touched him, sometimes saying, you and you when she was tired and wanted to let him know she would, all he had to do was ask, but not tonight. Tonight she wasn't feeling well.

"But yes," she said to her father. She was always saying yes to her father, and only when she was away from him did she wonder: does this make sense, her father? Driving all the way to her and home again and to her again in a night, driving to where she worked and waiting for her in the lot until the morning.

"It happened," she said to T. "I get confused."

She said, "But I like what I'm doing. I wanted to be in something hard. I wanted to be up all night."

"You're so fucking out of it," T said, and all the other boys said, too. "How do you know one man from another?"

The heavy-lidded eyes, the brittle hair and color of her

father: first off, these things, and his voice she knew. The juicy sweetness of his voice when her father was drinking, the way even the words came unbuttoned, the way he said her name, she could be flattened by this much about him.

And the money he gave her—and why not?—presents between the covers of oversized matches: Don't strike in gold from O'something's bar.

"Are these from us," she asked her father, holding up matches. "Have we been here?"

"You," she said, in the car again, free to speak and ready—even her earlobes oiled, every part of her clean and cleaned. She could get off looking at her arms. "I don't understand," she said. "What are you doing with a wife who beats you?"

"Oh," her father said, and he was sad, or he was tired. Hard to give it up, the look out onto water, some place to go. Neighbors far apart on either side—not seen until the winter, then sighted in the forked spaces, women standing at windows waiting to be seen. "But it is hard to see them," her father said. "The glare hurts my eyes, and the bog of common plants—the sappy heart-shaped, greeny danglers—beads the windows. Nothing happens, besides," he said. "I don't know why the wife is jealous."

She said, "The light in rooms like that puts me to sleep. I know the daughters," she said. From schools and summers, diving for soap chips in the boathouse, three or four of them, she and the daughters playing to know what it felt like. The winner held the soap between her legs the longest—Oh, yes, she remembered everything about this game. The way it ticked inside of her. "I wanted to melt down soap," she said. "But all of us girls got to play," she said. "We all got to fold our hands over the burning part."

They switched places. Her father tipped the seat and shut his eyes. She said, "I'm my mother's daughter. I want more than others." The way it was for her to wake up in the morning: the reason you think you've been here is you've been here. "I don't want it the same," she said.

"Everyone I know is broke," she said. "The night shift doesn't pay much. My boyfriends never work."

"And your mother?" her father asked. Grandfather and uncles making housecalls on her mother and scolding the poor woman before they made it better, every day less charmed by her mother, opening their wallets, saying, This has got to stop. There is only so much we can take. "Do you remember at all? Do you remember her at all?" She said, "Nothing's changed."

Her father said, "I can't get excited when I think about your mother."

"I am shivering," she said, and he was too. She could see the cold in his shoulders and in her arms resting on his shoulders, both of them, she and her father, white, blue-white—November still, and the horizon cindered thin, burnt out, quite black. She put her bare foot against the window and said look, "Look at my leg." No-color sky, flattened grasses. After a while she said, "Is this doing anything for you?"

Her father smiled. He said, "I've had better," which made her laugh, his saying, when what did he know?

"Just ask me how many times," she said. "I couldn't tell you."

She said, "I'm always in love with someone."

Her father said he meant it, he was tired, and she put her hands on his face and felt the slack tiredness. Bristle grown in driving just to get away—a day, a night, another day, he said.

"We don't have to do anything," she said. "I can save it."

Her father asked her, "Do you think I look young, or do you think I look like some old guy who got his eyes done cheap?"

"Look at my feet," she said, parked near the boat launch to a lake they didn't know, iced-over, gray-white, no clear shoreline. "Look at the footmarks I've left on the window."

"Such feet," her father said, and he put his feet over hers.

"Have I told you this before?" she asked.

But T didn't answer, bapping pencils against her head and dancing to his made-up music.

Her father said, "Find some music."

"Not that," her father said. "And no to that, no, no," then he forgot about the music or was indifferent to it; she could stop at anything she liked.

"But do you like it?" she asked her father.

"Do you like this dress?" she asked. "These shoes?"

Her father said, "It's hard for me to see. My eye still hurts." So she drove again, and she told her father what it was as they passed it, and in what connection to him: women at the end of narrow drives they passed. In drafty houses near the water, aproned Annes and pretty Susies. "You knew them," she told her father.

Her father said, "Did I?"

Her father said, "I don't miss many people."

She said, "I don't understand how you can stay with a wife who beats you." There, running her father down the hallway, a small woman with a small head and a racquet in her hand. Why did he stay with this woman, she wanted to know, and he never answered her, or not that she remembered. What could he have answered, besides, married to a woman such as this: marigoldy hair and bright mouth. After all those daughters, the wife still blushed. Some sweet name flicked loose from the roll, a Cathy, a Jane, ring guards clanking on her finger.

    She said. "You should live with me."
She said. "Maybe you don't want to know this, but it doesn't take much." And she was talking numbers—two and three a week, once that many in a day. "And I'm not very big," she said. "A bigger woman could take more."

"Once, here at the park," she said, driving her father slowly through the main streets of the town, pointing out where she had been. And here, the last time, with some doper—boots and lots of hair—the two of them on the roof, overlooking the entire fucking wayward county. She said, "Oh, Dad, anyone with what we had could have seen everything, too." Mother and one of her guys in her Mustang or her Bronco—the woman turning in cars as fast as she did men—grandfather and the uncles honking close behind. Keep your wallet shut, sign nothing, say you don't speak the language. She said, "What do I care about these guys? They're not looking out for me."

"I know who lives there," she said, and she pointed to insinuating driveways, raked gravel, money. She told her father she was easily coaxed into cars, at times even asking for it, waiting in obvious places for something to happen, in bedrooms and bathrooms, at doorways with lots of traffic. She said, "I can be dumb sometimes. I don't always know what I am thinking."

Look at the shoes she wore and the dresses.
Mother's mother still sewing flaps on the cups of her brassieres, so she would look flat, more boy-girl than girl, as if that were going to change things, as if there weren't other ways to it. "I know lots of ways," she said to her father. "Look," she said, and she lifted up her shirt. "Look at what the lawn did to my back."

She showed her father something else that she had brought, but he said, "No." Her father said, "I don't feel like it today."

T said, "The shit you deal wears off too fast."
"What do I care?" she said. "There are always men somewhere with money. I've got my grandfather, remember. I've got my uncles."

A friend of a friend had a place for them to go in a big enough town where a lot went unnoticed, but her father said, "No. I don't feel like it today."
"No," her father said. "No, I have no place to keep it. Just let me kiss you," he said, which she did. Arms crossed and eyes shut tight in the cold of the car, she moved a little closer to him and waited for the blow. **Q**

CHRISTINE SCHUTT

See If You Can Lift Me

I walk around to the other side of the bed we are sharing, and I put my face up close to hers and say, "Ann, please. Please," I say, and her eyes open, and Ann sees me, I think, and she says, "Sorry," in a loud, steady voice, and she knows. She knows she has been talking in her sleep. In the morning, she will ask, "Did I scare you?"

The dog, sleeping next to Ann, sleeps through it all. Good, loyal dog, this dog and all the others, for as long as I have known her. Ann holds the dog so close, I itch just looking at her bare arm slung around him. The bareness of it, that is what snags me, and how she wears these slippery nightgowns—must be cold. Her arm, around the dog, looks very cold and white and dry to me. The dryness especially—I notice this, in contrast to the tops of her breasts, where the skin, I think, is damp. No matter what Ann says, anyone would want to touch her here, but Ann tells me no, only the dog keeps her warm.

Ann says, "You do not know my kind of loneliness."

Ann says, "You have a child."

And so I have.

I used to say my skin smelled of girl from so much touching of my own. Ann remembers. Ann says, "That's when I got my pooch," and she takes his head up in her hands—Ann does this all the time—and chuffs behind his ears.

Or else she says, "Don't get near me. I smell of dog."

I cannot smell a thing. In this bed again, on my back, I am not near enough to anything other than me; Ann is turned away. She is tucked against the dog, dog pressed against her hollows, which isn't the right word for Ann there. Ann is full there. Ann can take hold there, and sometimes does, slapping herself in that place, which, when I am pressing on my own bones, I think of as hollows. The word is "hollows," but what I see is the flatness of girls.

I see cow skulls.

I see hurtful blue sky and desert, cholla in bloom, places I have never been to but sometimes think I would like to live in with Ann: New Mexico, Arizona, parts of California. We talk about living in these places. Ann says she can see us now at a long table, feeding lots of children. We are feeding some women like ourselves, and some men, too. This part makes us smile, Ann and me, talking about all the people we will feed. "And not only that!" Ann says. "Not only that. You can buy your girl a horse. Think about it," Ann says.

I do.

I lie next to Ann in this bed and think about us in the houses Ann says belong to grown-up friends, houses with rooms unused for days, houses with two and three of everything, blenders and televisions—closets full of coats of every size. I think about Ann with a man in such a house and doing some of the things she has told me she once did with a man, and I have done, too. I think about breasts—his, hers, mine. I think hard on these breasts, or else my mother's breasts come into view, long and unmuscled, and sometimes my grandmother's breasts or my grandmother's shoulders or the way my grandmother hitched up her brassiere to show off her strapmarks to me. My grandmother's shoulders are polished knobs of bone and smell of—but I can only see the cream she is using.

Ann's drinking, now this is something I begin to smell. I put my face into the back of her neck and shut my eyes and see the booze wavering off her arm like the oily heat that rises off the roads we hope to drive flat-out and sober.

Some team we would make.

Ann drinks through much of the night and likes to eat bread for dinner. She picks at the soft center and dangles the crust for the dog. "I wish you would eat something, pooch," she says; or else to me, "Are you sure?" Ann's nails are the off-white of old candles or honey. They are not always clean—from keeping her hand on that dog all day, taking that dog with her everywhere. I understand that she is tired, but I do not eat her food.

Sometimes Ann says, "Let's have cookies for dinner."

She says, "We are too old to be living like girls!" and we laugh because we *are* girls.

We are eating cereal at midnight.

We are sleeping together in the big bed and keeping a space between. We are still as stones, I think, and dumb as only girls are dumb to how most anyone wants it, someone's breathing.

Ann always says, "Stop looking at me," when I am looking at her, and she pinches me, but I go on looking, smiling this big, dumb smile.

I am smiling now.

I am thinking of Ann.

I am thinking of all the women I have seen stepping out of water. Mother, grandmother, sisters, cousins, all different, some remembered. Strong white legs and a black sex worn like a shield; I remember the impulse to kneel. I wonder, Is my cousin still red, and how have men treated her? I look at the way Ann sleeps, curled up against the dog. The last man Ann knew left her with sores. "What a dirty trick!" is what Ann says.

My mother again; I see her, hoisting up her pantyhose. She is saying, "Is that all you girls think about?" She is getting dressed or undressed or standing at the sink. Mother is saying, "It has been so long since, the parts are grown together." And that is how it looks to me, my mother's smeared gray sex, my grandmother's bones.

Sweet Jesus, I am cold.

Just looking at Ann, the blanket only to her waist and the rest of her pressed to the dog, makes me cold. How can she sleep like this?

"It is cold under the sheets" is what I tell Ann, but Ann says, "We are not in college anymore. We are grownups," Ann says. "We sleep under." Then she asks me—she does this—for a pillowcase, maybe from last time? But I am sleeping on last time's, so I give her new, and she hardly sleeps on it, she sleeps so close to the dog.

I shut my eyes and listen for sounds of her, but the only sound is of the dog. The dog is the noisy one. I have heard the dog talk right along with Ann, who lies so still now I must lean to feel her small adjustments, elbowing a pillow, pulling close the dog to warm herself, as Ann says she wants to warm herself against a person, someone, anyone else, then she laughs at herself. She says, "What an embarrassing story."

"Yes," I say, now lifted on my arm to see if she is sleeping. "Yes. Please." **Q**

CHRISTINE SCHUTT

The Summer After Barbara Claffey

I once saw a man hook a walking stick around a woman's neck. This was at night, from my mother's window. The man dropped the crooked end behind the woman's neck and yanked just hard enough to get the woman walking to the car. I saw this and saw rain winking in the yard in the light around our house.

Our house has the streetlight.

Mother says, "Our house marks the start of this corny town," and the two of us laugh at what it takes to be the start of something.

Here is the house at night, tall and white and waxy. And in the morning here is Mother, first one up by hours and already in a swimsuit and weeding muddy beds on her hands and knees. She has mud on her back and in her hair, and streaks have dried behind an ear where Mother says she has been scratching. Her arms are scored with bleedy cuts, nails mud-dull and broken, and there are mean-looking bites on her back, white swellings she must not feel or will not yet give in to touching, brave as Mother says she is to get hold of what she wants. I have seen shaggy weed ends spooled around my mother's hand rope-tight. "But look," she says, and wags off dirt from balled-up roots the size of shrunken heads.

This is what I have found to show Mother from the garden: one of a pair, dime-store flip-flops, size large.

Mother frowns at it. "Not his," she says. "This last Jack didn't have feet."

"Garbage, then," I say, like all my other finds, an upper plate of teeth, scarves, umbrellas, pens, and once, in the middle of the driveway, a ruined shirt so flattened by the weight of cars driving over and over it had taken on the shape of a dead thing, and I carried it to Mother on a stick.

Mother is still on this last Jack and on all the things about him that were missing. "For that matter," she says, "this last Jack didn't have hands." She says this with her hands under cold water, cutting off the ends of flowers. One end pellets off the wall, then rolls under the kitchen table. I watch where it goes, but I will not pick that up, please.

No, Mother.

No telling the things under there—oily tacks and combs, bread crusts and withered peas, always more, and furred with such a dust that I think they come alive at night and breed.

Mother says, "Don't be such a ninny, go and get it."

But no amount of teasing will send me looking for the bits of flowers that fly out in her wild cutting.

"You put your scissors up too high," I tell my mother.

I tell her something else she may or may not know: how we used to stand in line for it, me and Barbara Claffey, shivering in our new bodies and waiting our turn for instruction. Barbara Claffey swore the last Jack used his tongue.

Mother doesn't believe this story. "So where was I?" she asks.

"Chawed grass," I say. "That's how he tasted."

Mother smiles at me. "Just be glad you were there," she says. "You're probably smarter for it."

In and out of doors, I slug around the morning in my baby-dolls. I have nothing to hide, I tell my mother, although I don't know what to play with anymore.

Mother says, "Bored, bored, what's to be bored about?" and she moves from room to room, hitching rolled papers under her arm, clacking glasses in her grip—two, three, swiped off her bedside table in a motion. She uses water on the table and her nails to get up bottle rings of cough syrup that she says makes her dopey but helps when she can't sleep. Snaking the vacuum under her bed, Mother snorts up Kleenex. "Last night was bad. Coughing," she says, "and coughing."

"I didn't hear a thing," I say. Right through the streetlight's sudden extinction, the house went on sleeping with me.

Mother on her hands and knees, in the garden, is what I wake to, day after day, pressed out of doors by the midsummer heat rising in the houses of this hokey town. The Smiths across the street, the Dunphies next door; all the way to the end of the road, in what Mother calls a farm and Barbara Claffey calls a subdivision, are neighbors dressed in scant disguises. Too white, Mother says, or too fat for these clothes, but they don't know any better. Mother calls our neighbors hicks and winces when she sees Junior Klenk cut through our yard. Ready for a girl, she says, if he knew what to do with one.

Like that last Jack—he knew. Yipping the way he did that time in the yard when I saw him pricking Mother's legs with a weenie fork.

"Not mine," Mother says. "Some twangy girl's from someplace South. Watch out!" Mother warns. "The girls down there are dumb as foxes."

I think of us, me and my mother, in this nowhere town, in the flattened middle of the country, what do we know?

Barbara Claffey knows how to wad a pair of socks into bundles tight as baseballs.

"But does she know how to kiss?" Mother asks. Shuffling through bills and bills and more bills. "This is what I have to do now," Mother says. "I have to figure out how to pay for things."

I have nothing to do. Nothing, nothing long into the afternoon, with the morning just-remembered light rising in her room.

"No reason to panic" is what Mother says, and she looks over her shoulder as if expecting trouble, when all I want to know is what is there to do? "I've left things for dinner," Mother says, and takes up her glass and makes like this is coffee she is drinking, and she, a busy lady, elbowing the fridge, on the run, no time to talk, when she is talking all the time to friends in other, smarter towns. I sit between my mother's legs with my shirt hitched to my shoulders. "Scratch," I say. This way I don't mind when it is phone, phone, phone. This way, there is company.

"The tomatoes are alive," I say, in the kitchen again, worrying about my dinner. I lift off foiled lids to things she should have thrown away: jellied gravy, old rice.

"I can guess what you're thinking," Mother says, "but all that Barbara Claffey could do was fold cubed fruit in Jell-O."

I know how to mix drinks and make good scrambled eggs, buttery and smooth and not overstirred.

I know how to use a phone if one of us remembers a number.

"But there is never any paper," I say. "And where are all the pencils?" Not like when the last Jack was here and bringing home the pens he said he stole from office girls. Big on where to put things, that Jack, left and right, above, below. The boxed cuff links, the money clips, the sized and guttered coins at the front of the drawer he shared with Mother.

And the way that last Jack ate. "Remember?" I ask her. I used to pester him about the way he ate, leaving melon rinds scooped smooth as boat keels, or ears of corn with each pocket emptied yet unbroken and erect. How did anyone eat corn, I wanted to know, so that the cobs, stacked four and five high on the plate, looked like something you could eat again?

"Oh, Jack," Mother says. "The clean-plate clubber. His problem was, he didn't drink enough."

"And his handwriting," I say, and Mother scowls at me. She does not remember his lists. Cigs, bank, MSC? The loopy caps on his capitals or the evenness of his hand, word by word, line by line, on unlined paper. Only business, that Jack said.

The white in his hair—why white paint, what else? and the red in his eyes, just red string. I believed him.

Mother says, "He only looked like some big deal."

Under the kitchen table, I licked this Jack's plump shoes, both. But neither tasted of anything I knew of.

"Look," Mother says, and I can see her looking out from the crack in the door she leaves open when she pees. "You can always lock the door."

My mother soaping her throat is what I hear and soaping the ledge along her throat where she sometimes lays her hand when she is quiet.

"This is the plan," she is saying. "Someone handsome is on his way here. His name is John," my mother says, "but we know what that means."

Black hair, I think, buzzed to a shadow at the back of the neck.

"This new Jack is different," Mother says. "This new Jack has some style. Not like the last Jack, with his surf and turf or turf and surf—whatever the shit, on your first big date. Here's style for you, the last Jack's idea: snifters of candy on every table. What a dunce!" Mother says, handing me her puff and powder, showing me her back.

I white out trails of water leaking from her snarled hair.

"I know about a lot of things," Mother is saying, "but I do not know about men. Only this," Mother says, stepping from the damp and powder-traced impressions of her feet. "This last Jack had no taste. This last," Mother says, "I dressed him. Remember the suits?"

I remember coats, gray and odorless, square-cut and severe—the same, the same, shrilling on the closet rod.

"The cashmere sweaters?" Mother says. "In case he read a book."

I remember hats—not stiff, not Grandfather's hats, those upside-down coffins, but soft hats slumped at ease.

"Jack and his cheesy act," Mother says. "But he was handsome," Mother says. "I got carried away."

. . .

All those ties my mother bought him—so many, a ladderwork contraption looped with ties, one over another, sometimes slipping loose, falling in a faint behind the shoe racks. I have found these ties in the back of Jack's closet and used a broom handle on them.

"Do you have to go out?" I ask Mother, and I follow her from room to room.

"I have to think," Mother says, putting on her model's coat, looking through her closet. Dressing for this new Jack as she did for all the others takes up lots of time, she says. The purses packed like eggs, the mixed-up shoes all hooked in sacks.

"Better to be small," Mother says, taking out her slimming skirt. "Men take care of small women."

But I may grow to be as big as Mother. I have her hair, and what I think were once her eyebrows.

"And the rest?" Mother smiles at me.

"Takes two," she says.

I do not have my mother's face, that much I know. I do not have the face my mother wears for all her Jacks, smooth and lit up and amazed. Beautiful, the Jacks all say, and she is. I have seen women stop to look at her, my mother, and sometimes even ask, have they seen her before? Have they seen this face in magazines, the same face my mother pulls at now, pinching up her eyelids, saying, "I may be too old for this business."

"So why do you want to go?" I ask, watching the light wash over Mother's laid-out clothes. Slip, panties, pearls, and dress, all the whites turned yellow as old teeth.

"What do you think?" Mother asks, pouting at the mirror.

I say, "I think you shouldn't wear that dress. And don't let this John know you have any money."

Mother says, "Okay, little mother. What should I wear?"

"I don't know," I say. "Just stay buttoned. And don't tell this guy about me," I say.

Mother says, "I'm not listening to you."

"Remember the last Jack?" I say.

"Oh, that bastard," she says, "but what do you think he was doing to me?" She is penciling eyebrows, arched and alert. "Yes?" Mother asks. "I'm waiting," and she rubs off an eyebrow in the harsh way she did when this last Jack was here and she was always washing, saying she smelled bad—and Mother did not smell bad.

Night after night, dinner on the porch at the glass-topped table, me between the two of them, this last Jack and Mother, I sometimes got the smell of her confused with food and snatched her wound-up lipstick once and bit her red in half. I remember.

Under the glass-topped table, I saw my mother's long brown legs crossed at the ankles, thucking her heel in and out of her shoe.

" 'Do you think everything you do is so pretty?' this last Jack said." I ask, "What did he mean by that?"

"Who cares?" Mother says. "He made me feel dirty, that Jack." She licks a paintbrush to a point and outlines her mouth. Mother says, "Oh, God, I have no taste in men. Do you know what that means?"

I think.

I think I do—hearing how it was this last Jack came home. The plak-plak of his briefcase, open and shut; no other word for days.

Mother says, "He was not nice, that Jack."

I say, "So why are you going out?"

"Because I am," Mother says.

And she is standing now, my mother, in the spatter of her dress—back, forth, back, forth—a sweater, a purse, an umbrella in case. "Besides, I am hungry," Mother says, "for surf and turf—who cares? I won't be paying for this stupid meal, and if the man has any manners, I won't know the price."

"Oh, don't go," I say.

She is watching from her window the man's approach across the lawn. "You can wave from here," Mother says in the voice she uses with the new Jacks, and I do.

I wave and wave, even though she is not looking. I wave at my mother muscling her own weight under this Jack's arm. I cannot hear what they are saying; it is quiet in this town.

But the neighbors must notice my mother and her Jack. Either side of us and across the street, the Dunphies, the Smiths, Barbara Claffey down the street must press to windows startled as by birds that swoop and mate so queerly close, I sometimes draw the blinds to them—but not to Mother. I am ready for Mother and her sudden turning to see if I am watching her, to see if I am paying attention to how she stands, tottering in her shoes, ankles gagged and tense and helpless— and Mother is not helpless. My mother is brave, I think, and her upturned face is shining. I see this, and see them both, these willful lovers, tilted away from the house, leaning hard into the night. **Q**

ELIZABETH EVANS

Blood and Gore

I live on Radial Highway, so the place I usually go is up Blondo to Fifty-sixth. I'm only telling you, since there's room for more. I go up Blondo, then left on Fifty-sixth, so I end up looking down on Happy Hollow Boulevard. That's Mondays and Saturdays. There I got the advantage of being up on a rise, plus the corner lots. A buddy told me the bushes the people in that neighborhood put in can run a thousand bucks apiece. On my corner, though, the old lady keeps her yard slick as a mole's back, and the one across the way's not half bad, either. If anything comes down the boulevard, I see it early, I hop right on it. Also, somebody's always working on the grass and trees up there. Chemlawn—you've probably seen their trucks—but lots use guys out of pickups, which means nobody never notices me.

Say, it's nice there! All the fancy brick. Hardly nobody comes out or goes in, which makes it almost like being in the country, except cleaner and with sidewalks. Once, just after Halloween, I seen a squirrel sitting on the old lady's lawn, eating a miniature Milky Way bar! Right in its hands! That was the cutest darned thing! If I'd a camera on me, I could have won a prize in the Sunday supplement, what do you bet?

The old lady has a humpback. I seen her when she put on a garage sale last fall. There were some real lookers poking around in the stuff there, so I got out of my truck and went up, too. One I got next to, I asked what did she think about some Christmas lights they had there. Did she think they'd work right? That sort of thing. If you stood just so, she had on a big shirt and you could see between the buttons. *She* didn't know! She went on talking to me, fishing around in a box of kitchen things. "So," I says, "you live around here or what? You live in one of these houses?" That spooked her. Off she sneaked, over to the card table where the humpback and her friends were taking the money. All them looked at me real quick, then pretended they hadn't. That was the day I picked up my power drill. Black & Decker. Runs like new. I was set to pay for it—it even had the bits that come with it—but when I got near the pay table, the ladies sort of looked away. What the hell, I figured, and I took the drill out to the truck. Five bucks was all the old lady wanted for it. That's not much.

The garage sale would have been back when I got off Saturdays. Everybody at work who didn't have Saturdays wanted Saturdays, they had to have Saturdays so they could haul their boats to the lake. All them boohooed, Saturday, Saturday. I never could see anything so hot about Saturday. I couldn't sleep in Saturdays, with the cartoons on, and if I got up to watch, a pack of kids sat on me, a lot of peed pants ruining the start of a day their mother was going to turn to pure hell anyway, with talk of chores and so on. Finally, over break one day, I says—casual, since I mostly keep clear of them at work—"If there's trouble for the other fellows, you know, I could take Mondays instead."

Let me tell you, they about spilled their thermoses. Then, real quick, all them settled back like they hardly heard what I said. "That's real decent of you, Eule," they said. "Maybe one of us can make the switch." Shit for brains is what they got, while I got me a quiet house Mondays, and Saturdays I sneak out while the rest sleep and I look around a little before work.

Women in my neighborhood don't run, which is just as well considering the rear ends on most. If all them started to run, they'd bust up the concrete. Also true for the wife. She got the idea I should be in with her when the last one was born. Blood and gore. That put me off sex, believe me. That's birth control number one.

But what I started to tell: Last Saturday, I went out to look around before work, and something happened a little different. I went down the hill for the first one okay. I had things timed so I got to the corner just about the time she did. I stopped a little into the crosswalk so she'd have to go around me. This one was hefty, and when she come around the front of the truck, I said, real slow, "Hip-po." She got all red in the face, which gave me a laugh. Then I drove on past her, down Happy Hollow. I waved to her, like I'd just happened to be passing through. I always do that.

Then I drove back to Blondo, and around again. When I got to my lookout, though, the old lady's yard man had parked his truck wrong and screwed up my view! I almost missed what came down the street next, which is what I was going to tell you about. This one was a college girl. University T-shirt and shorts, fancy running shoes. Ponytail. Just in time I rolled down to the stop, and I called to her: "Say there!"

She acted a little spooked, but not so bad as the first. This one knew she was cute. I tooted at her when I drove past. She kept looking straight ahead, real snotty.

After I got parked again, some kids come by carrying poles. Where do you suppose they catch fish around Happy Hollow? I get bullheads out by Boystown, but I think those boys were dreaming if they meant to catch fish in the creek there. I drank coffee from my thermos and smoked a cigarette. I guess I fell asleep for a while. I don't remember doing that on a Saturday since I took Mondays. I don't have to start work till eight, but still, I was pushing my luck this time.

Anyway, I looked up, and here comes the college girl again, this time going the opposite direction, only now all pink and sweaty and tuckered out. To give her a start, I didn't turn my engine on, I just rolled down towards the stop. That truck can whisper when I want it to. The girl didn't even see me till I was in the crosswalk, and then instead of stopping or going behind me, like a fool she darted out into Happy Hollow!

Kaboom!

Up she went on the hood of this car going by, off she bounced. Instant blood and gore.

I set my parking brake and got out.

It was a guy in a yellow Trans Am that hit her—one of

those cars that was a real beauty maybe ten years ago but now it's all rusted to hell. You know what I mean. Nobody had taken care of that car at all. People who won't take care of a car like that don't even deserve to own it. A car like that—during winter, when they salt the streets, you got to clean off the undercarriage every time. You don't clean the undercarriage every time, there's your investment, poof.

Anyway, this guy from the Trans Am kneeled down by the mess he'd made of that girl. Her eyes were open but she wasn't going to be seeing nothing no more, if you know what I mean. Still, the guy goes, "Somebody call an ambulance!" He grabs at his shirt like he means to get in a fight with himself. "Somebody call an ambulance!"

Except for the yard men, people in that kind of neighborhood were mostly still to bed. An older guy was out walking his dogs, and these dogs—they were big dogs—they could smell that meat in the road. It was really something, believe me. It was all that old guy could do to keep the dogs back, and he was shouting at them, and kicking, and then the old lady with the hump come hobbling out.

"Oh, my Lord!" she goes. "I'll call! I'll call!" You should have seen her run! She wore this fancy pink bathrobe, all hiked up funny because of the hump!

The guy from the Trans Am sat there in the road, patting at the girl's head. Well. Jesus. I mean, part of it's over on the curb, if you catch my drift, and he's saying, "You ran right out in front of me! Didn't you see me?"

I went up a little closer. I don't like to get involved, but I tapped this one on the shoulder. "Hey," I said, "don't sweat, buddy. You got a witness, okay? I'm here. I seen it, okay?"

Later on, they put me in the paper. Did you see? In the end, the fellow didn't get charged with nothing, and I was the one that saved his neck. Just by being in the right place at the right time, I was the one who could come forward and set things to rights just by saying "I was there, and this is what happened." Q

DIANE HOPKINS

The Nipple of the Queen

It was a good day for greens—"blues," Eddie called them, but this was just to tease her. The stones were green, the same briny green as the waves that tumbled them up onto the sand and dragged them back, washed them in again, casting them into heaps with other stones: black, orange, gray, maroon, high on the beach where the sharp grass began, or stranding them singly, lone rocks lying wet and green near a nugget of red jasper or an egg of Maine granite—the beach spangled, the stones glistening, the tide ebbing in trickles around them.

They were serpentine, or so the man who used to run the rock store had told her years ago, almost twenty years ago, when, spreading a handful of gold and brown and green stones on the top of his glass display case, Ada pointed to the greens and said, "This is jasper, right?" It took the wind right out of her, hearing, "No, that's serpentine." It was deflating, like falling out of a swing when you were a child or having some adult say to you, "Pride goeth before a fall." She had always been afraid of that sin, the sin of pride.

Being wrong—but she had not been wrong, only mistaken, only misguidedly confident—somehow it had made her not want to ask what the other stones were: the polished browns whose black veins formed patterns like rivers and tributaries, the fine-textured golds with their grain like burled wood. Unusual stones, but none of them in her rock books, and now it was too late to ask; the store was closed and the man no longer there—retired or dead. The kind of thing that made you feel old.

"Well, you are old, sweetie," Eddie said, laughing at her when she said she was beginning to feel old (but she must tell him something to explain why she was so impatient these days, why she was snapping at him). And immediately, she wanted to contradict him: "No, I'm not!" Belligerent as a child. She was feeling more and more like a child; she was thinking more and more about childhood, and that was what old people did. She was seventy-two; that was old.

It was this gypped feeling that made her feel like a child. The impatience, too, a strange impatience that kept rising like an urge, like a tickling, as if she just wanted to get on with it, whatever it was, as if she had spent her whole life delaying.

It came over her at the worst times—when she was walking across a parking lot with Eddie, or when they were down here at the beach and it was one of his bad days and he had to walk so slowly. She should be glad he could walk at all, and she was glad, but it was like walking with her own grandfather and she a girl of six or so. That was what it reminded her of: his grip on her arm, so loving and yet so stern.

She had felt that same impatience back in June, when the house was overrun with grandchildren, everybody there at once: the three boys and their wives, all those little hellions running around making so much racket that even Eddie said, "I think I'm getting—what do they call it these days?—peopled out." She should have put her foot down and said no when the boys first suggested it. She should've told them Eddie wouldn't be up to it. And it was tactless, their coming from the ends of the earth, Texas and California and even France, as if they all thought this birthday would be Eddie's last, when even the doctor couldn't predict. But it was good of them, too.

Gypped. She had never felt like that as a child and never once until just lately. That was what made her snap at Eddie, snap at that poor little devil Claude, who knew no better than to dump out all her jars of rocks, the sorted ones. What a mound they made on the closet floor, all the greens and blacks and her few golds, years and years of sorting by color, by size. Her small rocks, so hard to come by on this beach; none of them was larger than a navy bean. But what was he doing in her closet, and how could she help being angry?

She didn't want to snap at Eddie. She wanted to question

him, and that was like a child, too: Why had they done this and not that? Why had they come here always in August when they could have spent the entire summer, and why had they never considered renting a place, or even buying? They always stayed in the motel. And then went back to Connecticut, where the weather was hot and muggy and she wished her life away, longing for fall. They could have stayed here, where the cool breeze blew straight off the Bay of Fundy and you could still get a twenty-five-cent cup of coffee at the little place in town where they always ate lunch. Other summers they could have stayed here. Not now.

She hadn't thought they would come, hadn't even dared hope. But Eddie said, "I feel much better, and we're going. I have to see what's on the beach."

His red jasper. He picked up nothing but red jasper, and all red jasper was his. Oh, she could keep the maroon kind, but not the bright reds, rosy, carnelian, the Chinese reds, Venetian. And the stones with the scarlet flecks so dense, so close together, that you could hardly see the dark matrix, those were his, too; they looked crazed, as if baked. She had hated to see the kids playing with them, the huge brandy snifter he kept them in tipped over on the rug. "Can I have this one, Grandpa? Can I have this one?" Of course he said yes. Then there were red stones in the lawn and underneath the sofa cushions; she was still finding them in July. What did children care about red jasper?

The rocks—each one different, each dry stone with its minuscule seaprint of salt rime, whorls that disappeared in the collecting bag, to reappear, patternless, a dusty film that needed to be wiped off when she oiled the stone's surface, bringing out the color; she used Nivea. Already she had gone through the jar, a small jar, that she had brought with her.

"Room smells like a funeral parlor."

She noticed he hadn't said that this year. He had always thought she should get a tumbling machine, but that made the stones look artificial, like plastic.

"You ought to do like me," he would tell her, rubbing a red stone up across the bridge of his nose, down, following the contour of the nostrils, his glasses lifting, unhitching themselves. It was a wonder they never broke; he would grab at them but not always catch them. They would land on the stones he had emptied onto the towel, to keep the sand off the bedspread. The hollow clicking of plastic against stone was so familiar that she didn't even need to turn her head to see the white towel, the red stones, the escaped glasses that looked both roguish and abandoned. In the light from the table lamp, his hair was blond gossamer, and that unsettled her, because in his youth his hair had been very dark and then, later, white but always thick; and not until chemotherapy gave him the angelic baldness did he begin to look to her like a stranger, for which, heaven help her, she could not quite forgive him. But he still had something, a radiance. Waitresses smiled at him, extra-warm, checkers in the market, too, and women strolling along down here with their own husbands—campers those people usually were, with RVs parked in the woods beyond, though for the most part, as today, the beach was empty.

"Blue," he called back to her, and she said, "Where?" then, "I see it," as if she didn't see several, all of them too large but still too beautiful to leave. You could think of yourself as being on a kind of rescue mission: saving the stones from being pulverized into sand. Of course that was foolish, and someday she might bring back the ones she hadn't needed or could bear to part with, though how could she bear to come to this beach again? She would go to the beach in California that Ed Jr.'s wife had told her about, where you could find moonstones (they were probably agates, not moonstones, but no matter). "How big are they?" she could hear herself interrupting, because Judith was already telling her about another beach, close by the first one, maybe an hour's drive, where you could find jade and the sand was black. A strange question—

she could see Judith thought so—though perhaps no more strange than hiding the wooden bowls full of special stones in the cupboards under the window seats; but there must be no more scenes, no more dreadful scenes. Poor little Claude. She must have terrified him: "No! Those are Grandma's!" His mother rushing in, fierce and stricken: "What has Claude done?" But nothing, nothing, a child of three. Judith, mystified, echoing, "How big?" as she plucked a stone from this or that bowl, fingered it. Judith in the window seat, the bowls beside her. So perhaps it had not been a mistake, succumbing to temptation, showing Judith the stones. "Come visit," Judith said. "Come next summer." But what did that mean, whom was she inviting? Surely she must know that Eddie was not up to much travel. It had taken them three days to drive up here instead of one.

At least, Ada thought, bending down, picking up the green stones, wiping the sand off on her sweat pants, at least she had not said anything ghastly, anything incriminating; she had not said, "Why, I'd love to come."

But she would love to, for somewhere she would have to find the small white stones for the pharaoh's gown, the small golds for the arms, for the legs, more blacks for the hair—like stiff strings of beads. She had enough greens for the gown of the queen. She must look at more pictures; perhaps both breasts were bare. But perhaps only one—she wasn't sure. Frescoes in tombs: all the heads in profile. But the torsos full front, then the legs from the side. Six legs crisscrossing, showing through the skirts. Herons in the foreground, long-legged ibises.

Pay attention, she told herself, giving her head a shake as if to dislodge water. Eddie was thirty, forty feet ahead of her, almost to the fish weir, and that was as far as they ever walked. He wasn't wearing his cap, and he should be; his blue windbreaker billowed behind him.

"Put on your cap," she yelled, but she was downwind and he didn't turn around. Beyond him, the cliff rose high and dark, the beach curving into its base and spruce trees furring its top; they were foreshortened in a way she would have got wrong, her perspective was so rusty.

Ahead of her, in the dingy sand, lay a piece of red jasper that Eddie had missed, not a small one, either, and that wasn't like him, though when he had walked here, the water might have covered it; his footprints were no longer at the water's edge but upbeach; the tide ebbed so fast—an inch a minute, she thought it was; it must be about to turn. There was a point where the outgoing tide met the tide coming in, and what was that called? She had never known; perhaps there was not a word. She squatted down.

Yesterday he had missed a stone much larger than this one, and she'd thought it was because the tide was coming in, wetting stones that he had only seen dry. But red jasper didn't need to be wet for you to see it, and therefore how much more horrible for her to have teased him about it, holding it on her upturned palm as they sat across from each other at the table in the little restaurant. "Look what I found. I'll give it to you if you're real good." And his tired smile, forgiving and even wry. "Well, I'm too far gone to be anything but good, so give it here." She would simply slip this stone into his collecting bag when he wasn't looking.

But other rocks she could show him at lunch—the ones he called his "aerial photographs," rocks marked as though by islands or continents; and she saw one now, a flat green oval, mapped blue like sea meeting shore, like the coast of Maine itself. Once you were hunkered down, you saw all sorts of treasures that eluded you when you were standing up. She wanted to look in the piles of stones up near the beach grass, dig down; the smaller stones were all underneath, though why was that? It was like the sermon on TV that she'd been listening to before Eddie said, "Will you turn that thing off?" about the three men who grew potatoes and two of them sorted their potatoes, but the third man just threw them into his truck, and the potatoes sorted themselves as they were driven to market.

It was a sermon about different ways of sorting, she knew that much, and she didn't care about that, about what the point was; she'd never intended to listen to a sermon. Only, the big potatoes ended up on top—that was what was interesting; she would've thought they'd end up on the bottom, being heavier. It was the same with the rocks. Eddie would know why that was; she kept forgetting to ask him. She would ask him at lunch.

The stone was drying in her hand, and she licked it to bring back the color, her tongue tasting salt. He would cock his head, squinting, holding the stone up close and then at arm's length, deciding what the story would be. "Ah yes, I remember taking this one. We were over in Sumatra, or was it Brazil?" Always places the two of them had never been.

"Ada," she heard him calling as she pocketed the stone, slipping it in with the jasper, because why mix it up with her own stones and then have to search for it—she might not remember, might be tempted to keep it for herself. Even with her sweater on, she was chilly; the wind was picking up. Why didn't he have enough sense to wear his cap?

She pushed herself up, the breeze cold on her shins; with the toes of her sneakers she nudged her pant legs down, first one, then the other.

"You coming or what?"

She mimed: Put on your cap.

But he cupped his hand to his ear, so she yelled the words.

He shook his head, laughing—not hearing, she guessed, not understanding. She shrugged. The water between him and the fish weir was aglitter with sunlight, and she squinted, thinking she saw something out in the blueness that was deeper than the sky's—something dark and round, stationary; it could not be a buoy.

"A seal!" she said, pointing.

If he would only turn around, he could see it much better than she could. But he motioned her to come on, so she did, plodding toward him; her feet were cold. Yesterday she had tried to get him to look at a barge that was slowly passing in front of the island, Grand Manan Island; every summer they talked about going to Grand Manan. And he had not looked at the barge either—oh, maddening man! But still, she must talk to him gently, she must not snap at him. She had snapped at him only this morning.

He was walking on now, not waiting for her, and she squatted down again, seeing a green, seeing a brown; it was a good day for browns, too, though none of them would ever find their way into the mosaic; they were all too large. The small waves plapped in close to her feet, curling over on themselves, sending in a listless foam. It was lucky the tides had been right this week, low in the morning, so she and Eddie could get down here when the whole beach was exposed instead of having to wait until afternoon, the way they did last week; he was always too tired in the afternoon. She'd thought he was going to be too tired this morning. But this had been a good week, and she'd had no call to snap at him, seeing him so slow to get moving, still sitting on the edge of his bed when she came out of the shower and he was supposed to be dressing, seeing him slumped there like a doleful boy; he looked so old, and somehow that was all right for her but not for him. His arms were so thin and flabby, and when he was young you could not even dent the muscles, pushing on them with your forefinger.

"Why can't you wear those T-shirts I bought you?"

Was there ever anything more irrelevant? It should have been a joke, it had always been a joke, but it didn't sound like a joke when she said it. He had always worn those sleeveless undershirts with the V necks, "old man's undershirts," she used to call them, as if she could get him to change; he was changing before her eyes. But a joke, a joke between them, so to say, so that he could say, "Ah, I see you've gone and bought yourself some new dust rags." Then to snap at him, for no reason, as if she wouldn't have been glad to give up her life if it could have saved his, like Queen Alcestis and her husband, whatever his name was, King Admetus, except that they were both then saved by Apollo.

Maybe, instead of Egyptians, she should do Greeks.

But no, the hair, she could see the hair, and sometimes she found herself idly sketching the figures, planning; the queen would be the central figure. The stones could be glued on a backing of masonite, a large square of it, or else Plexiglas.

A wave foamed in up around her feet, rising over the toes of her sneakers, and she said out loud, "Damnation." Now Eddie would want to go back to the motel so that she could change her shoes, and she did want to look in the piles, where, long ago, they had seen a man with a walking cast sitting in the stones that were warm on top, cold underneath; his crutch lay there next to him. The very picture, she told Eddie, of true determination, or else pure greed. They had spoken to him, and he had said, "I'm getting these for my daughter." No doubt he was telling the truth, and she shouldn't have laughed, saying, "That's a lame one if I ever heard one," because then Eddie was exasperated. "Do you have to say everything that comes into your mind?" As if she did. Only, if everyone took as many stones from the beach as she did, someday there would be no more, because there could not be an infinite supply, and where did they come from, anyway?

Another wave washed in. She thought: I should move. But it was too much trouble to move. A tiny fragment of red jasper eddied in the foam, and she rocked forward, making a dam of her hand, the slurry of icy grit numbing her fingers so they opened, the water rushing through and the fragment as well, she was afraid, because now it was nowhere to be seen; there were just bubbles quickly collapsing on the sand's surface as if they had been sucked dry from underneath. She dug down, wedging the sand aside with the heel of her hand; it was like digging for a vanished crab. But then there it was, and not where she was digging but simply lying on the surface, an almost perfect red circle; it must have been under a bubble. She had found the nipple of the queen!

"Ada!"

Over the waves she could hear the stones in his canvas collecting bag clinking together as the bag swung against his leg. He had given up and come back for her, and she wished he hadn't.

She stood up, dancing back stiffly before another wave could get her. "Now, don't go scolding me." He had put his cap on; at least he had put his cap on. "Look, there's a seal," she said, pointing with the arm he'd been about to take. And there *was* the seal; it had appeared as soon as she had spoken, as if by magic, and submerged as she pointed, so it was gone when he turned around to look.

"Well, there *was* one."

He frowned. "How do you know it was a seal?"

"I saw it before. It was watching us."

"My dear," he said, humoring her; he had always humored her. He had always asked, "How do you know?" and she had always hated it.

"I saw the whiskers," she said, though she had not seen the whiskers. "Well, I did," she said, shoving her hand into her sweater pocket, poking the queen's nipple down into the fuzzy seam. She wanted to look in the piles; she was too tired to look in the piles. "Are you too tired to look in the piles?" she said.

"No," he said. But he was too tired—she could see it, see that he was more tired than she was. "I'm fine," he said, linking his arm with hers.

He steered her up the incline to the heaps of stones, pod-shaped and flat, their ends tapered by tides that would not be that high again until winter. He was a man, she thought, who would not have begrudged her the whole beast. And she felt herself melt, as she always had, and heard herself concede:

"It could have been an otter." **Q**

TERESA LEONE

Sandwich

Wednesday. Thursday. And then possibly Friday. She marked that down. No thought of Saturday.

"Hi," he said as she let the cat in the door.
"This is the cat," she said.
"Oh."

They walked along the sidewalk side by side. He thought about his car and which one it was. He remembered a blue one somewhere. Somewhere, someone he knew had a blue car. It was kind of small and had doors that locked by pushing a button. Sometimes the doors were ajar. He liked that car. It must be somewhere parked on a road, he thought.

She had her head down. Her arms were folded across her chest. With clenched hands, she held the opposite collars of her old musty coat. Her hat was pulled down over her eyes. The curls of her dark hair sprang out from beneath the hat in little uneven spurts that bounced up and down as she walked.

Tuesday . . . Maybe Tuesday, she thought. Wednesday seemed certain. She stopped walking and tapped her bottom teeth with a bent, thoughtful finger. And Thursday! she thought as she caught up to his pace again.

"Yes," he said. "It might very well be in a garage."

"I won't even think about Saturday," she muttered. She shook her head with determination.

Saturday popped into her head. She thought about it. Something was happening Saturday. She would not think about it. She pushed it out of her mind as she bit her lower lip and looked ahead.

The blender his mom had was blue. It had five buttons. He remembered pushing the first button. It was a long time ago. He watched his sandwich spin around. The next button went faster.

  The street was wet and dark. He saw something, though. It was his car. Red. His car was red. Not many accessories, though, he thought.

"No carpet, for instance," he said as he opened the car door.

She sat in the seat and her coat hung out of the door, keeping it partly opened. She took one arm out of her coat sleeve and let the rest of her coat hang from her other arm.

"The cat," she said, "is at home by the door."

Her mind clicked over to Thursday. Thursday and maybe Friday. Wednesday definitely. Yes.

"The button on your coat," he said. "I want to push it."

"Of course," she said. **Q**

SARAH CHACE

The Acts

Lamb of God, let me palm it off as a stirring text, and then go on. Let me close a girlish fist and hold it out for the size my heart was then. I have bargained away the pity of the parish already, used up the ready beds that I remember as the parish booths. My priests (or so I like to hear them, so I like to see them) will hear it with a stir, a stroke. My text no longer stirs them with its case for a girl made easy early. So when, my lamb, my listener, did this willing spread of flesh and bone and bread-and-butter breath take place? (And I was willing, I assure you.) In the Year of Our Lord twenty pleasing years ago. And where, besides in the palm of his starting, Jewish hand? In a room as big as a temple—in a room where I slept with his daughter—in the grinding dark, in the despairing light. His daughter had a seagulled shoulder and I had the joints of a parish thief. Lamb of God, I took him in.

Lord, I am not worthy. Let me land upon a rock, let me land upon my hatred of the Jews. Let me dig around for things to show you. Here I have the worthy, Jewish swell I feel in their helpless heat, here I have what he had me hold, here I have what he made me say in that starting dark I talked about. Here I have that Jap kimono.

They like to travel, I am told they like to travel. Let me go to Asia, where it started. Let me get you to that thwarted dark where I will wash your feet with all my dulcifying tears and dry them with my reconstructed hair.

At first I was so well received! And such a sorry *Liebchen,* darling, with such a lack of class for looks! My genes were bungled in the chromotinic mistake of my mother's mowed-up hair and her pinpricked skin, while my father waxed blessed with them both and my sister got them. I came to this assimilated, seagulled shoulder's house my tenth October. By ten o'clock (a Sabbath Friday night) I was doing things already for this friend, this half daughter of Zion, in an ornamental orphan's dance—a choreographed, balletic effort. The freckled daughter chose the music, I just slurred my feet across the floor the way a plain girl does. We danced for her father in those Jap kimonos (a trip to Asia in retirement: the grandparents in Japan), and after curtain and one sweaty-handed man's applause, I rested in the second master bedroom (I mean hers—I mean, the girl's), the daughter's guest the whole lamented weekend.

Did I mention that we did a feckless combination for her father in those sherbet colors, those bent kimonos, with nothing underneath?—and the talk that caused at school, the talk! Did I mention that my father was living in our home when I got there for the weekend, and broke the news he was no longer by the time he picked me up on Sunday on a sudden Sunday night?

Oh, holy night. It was a crime I did most often of a frigid Friday night. The daughter would sleep in her snapping feet-pajamas and her quilt, while the wife was in her Irish cups, or standing in her leotard, lifting business through the mail in a room that was somewhere else, well proofed against our sounds. It began, and it ended, too, by being quiet. I don't remember if I never liked it; O Lamb of God, I think I always did. On Saturdays, we watched cartoons, by God. Another year, and yet another Saturday (we were beyond cartoons by then, I think), I had my throat examined by her father in the hall with a tongue that tasted like a sand-apparent tomcat father's tongue—oh, older than my tongue by thirty years or so, I guess. He held my tightly striped and racy rayon blouse—long-bodied and lean—within his golfing arm within the foyer of the master bedroom. The girl—his daughter, right?—and I had had a fight about the trolls, I think. Anyway, that fighting afternoon he kept me in the house.

I am sure that such a spring day as this will one day lick my throat.

And the other nights, my darling, the other crimes? How many Hail Marys might they warrant? How many long Our Fathers? My head went looking for silence when I rested it for a minute on a loamy, looming shoulder within a field of poison ivy—which was the first decisive time with some coeval, or anyhow, within the silent ballpark of my teenage years.

This is how I faced myself, a little girl.

I was not lucky. You, my ready dear, I bet, were lucky. I feared the holy fathers in their booths, I saw their guns before I saw them. I forgot the words for confession except Forgive me, Father, for I have sinned. I lit the candles without permission of the Sisters of Our Holy Charity. I beheld my melting fear in me like magic sealing wax. One night, I broke her father's ivory rook. I wore a cape of camel's hair her mother loved; I broke no hearts.

My father was fooled—indeed, he was glad I had a place to stay on his assignment weekends. My gamine friend—*en fin,* she was protected, what? Her father bought us off with twenties in the hall. We went to school, we played like the plague. The twenties (when I took them, when I saved them) came in handy in the pinch of time we had in afternoons to spend beyond my means. I dreamed no dreams for years. Four years of this; I've counted several times.

Lord, I am not worthy to receive you under my roof.

About the time my skin broke out (and it was early, even for a broken girl), I met them all; I mean, my equidistant girl friends of the time. I met them through the sins of my father, at the fusing point of childhood, when I was nine and hungry, through the sins of my mother. The other part of our isosceles of semi-blooming, semi-teenaged girls (we were ten, eleven, twelve together; thirteen changed us all) was the daughter of my parents' young-eyed, moneyed friend, freckled with the genes of England. We went to musicals. We dappled in ballet. We failed at math together in silent failures; we were equally bad at French for all those broken years. I was the first with something aching in my chest that hurt me on my face-down bed, the first with something we all called fur.

And in the sixth grade—*in medias res*—after countless traps of sound in soundproof, wifeproof, dogproof rooms (the daughter had a Dane) were set while I was flunking French and leaning, in my mind, in the direction of my secret not my studies, I wound down, for a time, into an abscess of self-admiration—even though all there was to admire at this particular, visceral point were my balletic arms. And even then, and even so, my girl friends scolded me for vanity! The scolding came in the form of the daring game, entitled, What I Don't Like About You. They landed on my admiration in the daughter's mirror of my upper arms. I gave it up in public.

I still—I will not touch these men, with all their salted parts. They cower me, like trees that grow inside a house, unwanted things. They say, You are a little passive for such a daring girl.

When we were all thirteen, I gave myself to Tony until ten o'clock and then, at ten, to Sam. When I was fourteen, I lay inside a summer field of poison ivy for a brawned and brutal, soothing boy who had my golden heart, I thought, and then in August—some days later—I had his brother in my attic bed, behind a rock, below a low sea wall; and then, Oh Son of Man, I would light my flame of flesh for anyone at all. **Q**

DIANE DESANDERS

A Piece of the Angel

Here are Lucy and Cosette, not exactly on the top of the Montejo Hotel in Mexico City, but more like on the next-to-the-top floor in their three-room suite, taking turns screaming Spanish to the operator, trying so hard to get hold of Lucy's ex-brother-in-law, Octavio, wanting in the worst way to invite Octavio for drinks and for dinner later the same day up in the nightclub-restaurant, which is the thing that is peaceful and calm up there, that is all spread out up there, on the top floor of the Montejo Hotel—that is so complete in itself up there, with awning, bandstand, bougainvillea, palm trees—and with a lovely view of the Angel.

As we come upon them, we see Lucy, and we see Cosette, and we see the clothes and the reading matter and toilet articles and address books and used room-service dishes that Lucy and Cosette have dropped and have tossed here and there, and onto all surfaces, so that all of these constantly-being-accumulated and then sloughed-off belongings of Lucy and Cosette are now spread out all over their next-to-the-top-floor three-room suite.

You can imagine.

Lucy is the one slipping from but gripping the edge of the chenille-covered twin bed in the first room we come to, with the ragged phone book balanced open across her knees, with her plastic reading glasses sliding down her nose, with her lit cigarette trailing ashes that aren't falling into the heaped-with-lipsticked-butts glass ashtray that's edging haltingly toward her on the bedspread as if trying to get her attention in time.

"Octavio, we have to get hold of Octavio!" says Lucy.

Cosette says nothing.

Cosette is the one in the thin, skin-colored silk slip with

nothing else on underneath, the one who fans herself with the day-before's Sunday supplement from the newspapers still spread where fallen like low-slung Arab tents across the floor, the one who wanders in spool-heeled satin slippers, who holds up and considers first this blouse, then that jacket, then something else, then lets each one fall—the one who keeps on strolling from room to room and back, and who in each room keeps on looking out and leaning out all the open windows, who keeps on comparing all the different open windows' different versions of the not-quite-as-lovely-as-it-could-be, next-to-the-top-floor view—the trees, the avenue, the city—almost the Angel.

Cosette has had her turn on the telephone. And besides that, Cosette's Spanish isn't all that good—she is always finding herself unexpectedly speaking French is what she has been telling Lucy about it.

Cosette goes over to the table as if looking for something in particular, but not being quite able to put her finger on what it is, she picks up the bottle as if this will have to do, and Cosette freshens her Tequila Sunrise, stirs her Tequila Sunrise with the plastic palm-tree swizzle stick brought earlier by the room-service waiter with the blue but pin-pupiled eyes. Cosette had been saying earlier to Lucy that she had seen tiny-pin-dot pupils like that before. Lucy said Octavio's were not like that.

Lucy keeps on dialing.

"I thought you said it was never hot in Mexico City," says Cosette, her back to the room, her words spoken out the window as if she has not yet decided whether her words are meant to be heard.

"¿Hola? ¿Hola? ¿Señora? ¿Señora?" shouts Lucy in that voice of hers that has no problem with decisions, that is eager to get on to the next decision, and the next, and the next.

Lucy's hair is slipping out from its hairpins where Lucy keeps jabbing and stabbing her bitten-all-over pencil into the wound-up bun at the back of her head—as in newspaper days.

Lucy will definitely have to take down and comb out and then put up and slick back her hair all over again if she and Cosette are going to go up on the top floor for drinks and for dinner later on tonight. Lucy does not mind putting up her hair all over again—she does it all the time, with irreducible speed, and with much involvement of mouth and teeth, with bobby pins and elastic bands snapping.

"Life's too short!"—that's what Lucy says about the way she wears her hair.

Lucy and Cosette have only peeked in up there at the top floor, since they are of course saving the whole experience of the top floor—the bandstand, the palm trees—for the special occasion of drinks and dinner with Octavio—lunch having been slightly burned *quesadillas* at Sanborn's up the street.

After lunch, the two of them agreed on ordering the drinks to their rooms, on breaking open their own duty-free Cuervo Gold as well, and on settling down again with that operator again, on telling that secretary again—and also on calling Octavio's sister's house, on calling Betty Ann and Enrique, on calling Lucy's old boss, and then on trying to get someone at that number that used to be that old friend of Octavio's who might also know where Octavio's mother's new house is—Octavio being the one his mother depends on, says Lucy. And then if they could ever actually get that hotel operator again—who must be avoiding us again, says Lucy—then they could recheck all the other messages they had already left again.

"I wonder what other places we might try. There must be some other people—some other places—somewhere else we can leave messages for Octavio," says Lucy. "There must be something else," says Lucy.

"Octavio," says Lucy, "we have to find him—we have to find Octavio! Where is he? Where the hell is he?" says Lucy.

It's been three days.

And would you just look at this three-room suite without maid service! What a mess Lucy and Cosette have made in the three days they have been hardly-ever-leaving these two-bedrooms-and-sitting-room-bath, and have never picked up any of their clothes, their maps, their newspapers and magazines and brochures, their shopping bags and Mexican dresses, their postcards and hairbrushes and nail polish and liquor bottles and matchbooks and ashtrays and coffee cups and spoons, and—yes—and used underwear!

Lucy and Cosette are not all that ashamed of themselves for this mess, either, because—as Lucy keeps saying to Cosette, as Cosette keeps saying to Lucy—as soon as they do make contact with Octavio, as soon as both of them really do know for certain and without a doubt that Lucy's ex-brother-in-law Octavio—this very same Octavio about whom, ever since the first time the two of them met, Lucy has been telling Cosette how handsome and how fabulous and how really-something-special Octavio truly was. As soon as the two of them are able to feel certain that this same—and hopefully unchanged in any detail—Octavio really is going to be coming up here, then the two of them will hardly need to explain to each other or to anyone else about how excited and how inspired they will then be to go ahead and get busy and clean up and straighten up and fix up the entire three-room suite as nice as can be. This is absolutely for certain.

They will do their hair. They will do their fingernails and also their toenails. They will go right out and buy flowers for the rooms, and they will buy vases for the flowers for the rooms—and next to the vases filled with the flowers all around in the rooms, Lucy and Cosette will place the magazines and the maps and brochures on the tables in little fan-shaped, graduated stacks. It will be lovely—simply so lovely—as soon as Lucy and Cosette can determine the location of the eternally desirable Octavio. Where could Octavio be?

So here they are—the two of them—Lucy and Cosette. Are you imagining?

Lucy slams down the phone, tosses the Mexico City phone book across to the other bed, causing it to bounce and to fall in a ruined jumble over the other side of the other bed and against the wall, and causing the heaped-full glass ashtray to spill over onto the chenille bedspread of her own bed and onto her skirt. Lucy stands up, bending, brushing, calling names at the mess.

Cosette holds a leaf-printed scarf up to the window light, lets it fall, watches it spiral down. She does it again to watch the spiraling-down shadow on the wall next to the shadow of the jerking elbows, the bending and brushing figure of the complaining, name-calling, perpetual-motion Lucy.

Then Cosette spirals down herself to the floor, the way she once learned to do in an acting class. She does this in imitation of the scarf. Also of the shadow.

Cosette lays herself out on the floor. She turns onto her side, and she peers over and up into one of the newspaper-Arab-tents close beside her on the worn carpeting, as if she might be thinking about trying to crawl inside it.

Lucy looks over at Cosette on the floor, then goes to the door and starts stepping into her tennis shoes, which she had earlier flopped down there, one toe pointing directly to the other toe.

"I am going down there and talk to someone at that desk about that switchboard operator," says Lucy.

Cosette sits up on one elbow. "Wear your high heels," says Cosette. "Wear the red ones."

"If I can find them in all this mess," says Lucy. "Where did I put those shoes, anyway?" Lucy starts kicking newspapers aside, letting her stockinged feet rummage and scout across the room toward the windows.

Cosette jumps up, and while slapping her slippers in what could still be described as strolling, she beats Lucy to the window—goes to the table. "Are you finished with this drink?" she says, holding up Lucy's watered-down Cuba Libre, toddling it back and forth in the air in her hand.

"No, not yet," says Lucy, taking it.

. . .

Both women stand for a time, finishing off their drinks and looking out the windows. The sun isn't overhead anymore. The afternoon air is still. The ice is shifting in Cosette's glass, making little noises.

"If it wasn't for those trees there, I'll bet we could see the Angel from here," says Cosette.

"Yes. Almost. But not quite," says Lucy. She lights another cigarette, takes a long drag, producing a red flash quickly obscured by another long, flaking ash.

Cosette starts moving to the different windows again, looking out at the different views again, leaning out farther than before this time, looking back at the other windows at the front of the building, seeing if any comparisons can be made.

"But I'll bet we'll see it perfectly beautifully from up on top later on tonight after we get up there with Octavio!" says Lucy. "I'll bet the Angel itself could almost look over to the awnings and the palm trees and see us up there on top tonight—the three of us sitting up there—you, me, and Octavio!" says Lucy.

Cosette turns and moves away. Lucy flicks her ash out the window, follows Cosette into the other bedroom, where many amazing outfits—mostly Cosette's—are laid out on the bed in amazing combinations, Cosette having been the first person Lucy had ever seen wearing spike heels with rolled-down socks when the two of them first met in Paris at a lunch counter and wound up becoming friends after talking all night—Cosette telling Lucy about the time she had drinks under an awning with Marlon Brando when her sister was working on *Last Tango in Paris*—although it was impossible, Cosette said, for her to get Marlon's full attention.

Which naturally resulted in Lucy telling Cosette about the time she divorced her husband, gave away even her highschool yearbooks and Best Camper trophy, threw a duffel bag, a suitcase, a fox-trimmed coat, a typewriter, and a .38 pistol into her baby-blue 1967 Fiat and drove straight through from Houston to Mexico City, "back when the bribes at the border were only five dollars," to take a job with a news bureau down there.

The open suitcases of Lucy and Cosette are lined up—a row of oysters—against the walls in the second bedroom as if awaiting instructions—as if listening for the phone to ring, and for it to be Octavio.

Cosette takes the last piece of ice from the bottom of her glass. Lucy walks across to the window near Cosette in the second bedroom, and the two women stand, looking out again.

The much-beloved, much-photographed, gold-leafed Independencia Monument Angel, which spreads its angel wings like blessings high over the main avenue as if about to step off, as if about to any minute fly right off and out away from the monument—to fly up, and out over the city—can almost be seen from where they are now standing—but not quite.

Hints of its gleaming color flash, halo-arcing through the trees lining Paseo de la Reforma below, making it appear that the Angel might be moving behind the slightly moving trees, as if unstable on its high, one-toe perch—as if earthquake-shaking, as if tremor-toppling loose from base to plunge to earth the way it had plunged swerving to earth one night years before, into the street.

"And there'll be floodlights on it later tonight, after the sky turns dark," says Lucy.

Cosette is leaning out the window on her elbows now, peering through the trees as best she can.

"I know with all the calls we've got out for him, we'll get through to Octavio anytime now, and then he will call us back, and then we can call up there to the top floor, and then we can make our dinner reservations," says Lucy. "And we'll be sure to get a good table—to get the number-one best of the good tables, in fact," says Lucy.

She flicks her ash.

They both look out.

Above the trees the afternoon hum of the traffic river of old-model speeding bumper cars below hangs heavy at a certain level in the air, along with the low-gathering afternoon smog—the humming smog, the moving trees, the avenue-traffic river, all three sitting one on top of another like a three-layer Mexican sand painting spread out as far as the eyes of Lucy and Cosette are able to see on this particular day, standing here, looking, drinking, smoking, waiting, standing, looking, standing, waiting.

Lucy lights a new cigarette from the old cigarette, blows a long, straight stream of smoke out the window. She picks up the same ashtray Cosette had pocketed from the Hilton Ballroom before they had moved over here because of the Montejo's being more Mexicano—she balances it carefully on the windowsill, looks at it balanced there, at the ashes being pulled, floating, twisting, rising, out into the street air. She turns.

"Did I ever tell you Octavio had a piece of the Angel?" says Lucy to Cosette.

"A piece of the Angel?" says Cosette. "You're not going to tell me Octavio climbed up there!" says Cosette.

"No, no, he didn't have to do that—Octavio used to say the piece fell right at his feet—a gold-leaf, wing-tip piece that chipped in the fall when he was a kid," says Lucy. "People were all around in the street, he said, when the earthquake hit, and the Angel fell as though diving to earth—and the piece skipped straight over to him, like a shiny tiddly-wink—right before the crowd came running," says Lucy.

"Then what?" says Cosette.

"Then he grabbed it and ran!" says Lucy. "He kept it with him after that, always, like a charm—said he learned pretty early to be careful who he showed it to—said people were always trying to get it from him—said it made him see things differently—said it changed his life," says Lucy.

Lucy looks out. Cosette looks out. They both stand looking out, holding their empty glasses, both of them moving their empty glasses—Lucy rotating hers in tight circles, Cosette rocking hers, back and forth, back and forth.

"I wonder if he still has it," says Cosette.

"I'll bet he does," says Lucy.

"Probably he keeps it locked up safe somewhere by this time, if he does still have it," says Cosette.

"I don't think so," says Lucy. "He always said it had to be on him, for some reason—it was as if it was just in case of something. He always said he would not lock it up."

Cosette puts down her glass, pulls one chair up to sit facing another chair by the table next to the window, sits in it, lets one arm rest on the sill, then lets her arm trail out the window.

"So was it always so difficult to ferret out the whereabouts of this Octavio?" says Cosette.

"Well, not always, but sometimes . . . I mean, well, he was married to my sister, after all—and we were all close at one time," says Lucy. "We were all three very close," says Lucy. "Way back then," says Lucy. She sits in the chair opposite Cosette. "Well, maybe," says Lucy, "maybe." She is looking out the window. "Maybe," she says again.

Cosette puts one foot up on the arm of Lucy's chair. She leans and pulls another scarf off the table, this one printed with yellow suns. She holds it up to the light by two of its four corners, then looks over to see the shadow on the wall.

"When we get up there tonight," says Cosette, "we'll have to let Octavio take the best seat for the view—whichever seat up there he wants!"

"Yes!" says Lucy. "And we won't let Octavio get the check!" says Lucy.

"We'll grab it ourselves before he has the chance!" says Cosette.

"Yes, yes!" says Lucy.

"And we'll get a table near the bandstand," says Cosette. She is pulling the scarf into a long sash.

"And also near the wall," says Lucy, "for the view—for the best possible view of the Angel," says Lucy. "And all during dinner," says Lucy, "we'll be smelling the bougainvillea that is up there climbing along the top of the wall—that keeps on year-in-and-year-out-no-matter-what blooming along the top of the wall."

"Climbing and crawling and clinging along the top of the wall and over the sides," says Cosette, "stretching out vines and its purple flowers, reaching out and out, all along the top of the wall and over the sides," says Cosette. She is tying big square knots into the center of the sun-printed scarf-sash.

Lucy draws on her cigarette. She puts her glass on the table.

"And after they take away the dinner plates," Lucy says, standing, leaning with both hands on the windowsill, "we will all three stand up and look out together—you, me, and Octavio—we will all three go over to the wall, and we will all three lean over to see the bougainvillea trailing its flowers and its vines down the sides of the building."

"Down to where the neon Montejo sign is over the door down on the street," says Cosette.

"And there'll be people down there on the street—upturned faces," says Lucy.

"Outstretched hands!" says Cosette, stretching out her hands.

"To catch flowers!" says Lucy. "We will toss out flowers that will flutter and fall down through the air!"

"Yes, yes," says Cosette, "flowers we will all three pull loose and toss—flowers falling over and over through the air—the people holding out their hands!"

"And then Octavio—" says Lucy. She holds a breath.

"Yes!" says Cosette. "Yes! Yes! Octavio will take out that piece of the Angel!"

"That gold-leaf, wing-tip piece of the Angel," says Lucy. "And he'll toss it!" says Lucy.

"Yes!" says Cosette.

"To glitter through the air—to turn over and over in the air," says Lucy. "—to go down," says Lucy.

"To go down," says Cosette.

"Who will catch it?" says Lucy.

Cosette overhand-throws her yellow-suns knotted scarf out the window. It arcs out of sight.

"We won't know," says Cosette.

"Anyone," says Lucy.

The phone rings.

Lucy draws on her cigarette again, leans on the windowsill again, blows out smoke in big cumulus laughing-puffs that stand wispy-dissolving gradually around the edges.

The phone rings again.

Cosette pours more Cuervo Gold from the table into her Tequila Sunrise.

"Octavio, Octavio, we have to get hold of Octavio!" says Cosette.

They hear a knocking at the door.

At the window we see a glowing. **Q**

DAWN RAFFEL

Seeds in Public Places

What my mother is saying to me about pearls is that you must rub them against your teeth. "Like this," my mother is saying to me, demonstrating, moving an earring over her lowers. "Friction."

I am engaged to be married. The shoes are flat. The dress needs something else, my mother says, some accessory or accent. The veil could stand a press.

We are in my mother's master bedroom, where we are looking in my mother's box of jewels; at least, that is where I have been looking. Sun is coming through the windowpanes, showing up motes.

It is dazzling, too dazzling.

I have sometimes seen men turn and watch my mother walking on the sidewalk. I believe this happens often.

My mother says that she has always followed certain rules, which she has tried to teach to me: Break your rolls, powder your feet, don't eat foods with seeds in public places.

I love the things that sparkle in this box my mother has. I love the box, which is lined with ruby velvet.

"It's a trick," my mother is saying, "something a woman ought to know." My mother puts the earring back. I can see her lipstick on it. "If there isn't grit, it's paste," she says.

"If things we owned could talk," my mother said to me last week as she was teaching me to recognize the sound of fine crystal.

I watch my mother fiddling with a clasp. "These are real," my mother says, and holds the strand against my throat. "See? See how delicate? How right?"

But I am trying to pick out something shiny.

"Look," I tell my mother. "I think the dress wants something else."

"Listen here," my mother says to me. "Trust me."

I have my finger on a ring I used to notice on my mother's slender hand. It is an opal. "Go ahead," my mother says. "It's yours."

My mother has often told me not to mix gold with silver.

"They are knotted in between," my mother is telling me. "They can be restrung," she says. "See the subtle luster?"

She says, "Really, you should give a thing a chance.

"Just this once," my mother says.

"Never mind," my mother says to me. "Forget I mentioned anything." She starts to ball the pearls up in her palm, and this action makes a noise.

"Mama?" I say.

"What now?" my mother says. **Q**

DAWN RAFFEL

Something Is Missing of Yours

They are burning the leaves out back, at the edge of the yard where the yard meets woods—far back enough for the father's peace of mind from the house. The father, of course, is the one who is taking care of the burning. The daughter, having done her share of raking and bunching, is standing aside in the shrubby bramble, hands slid into her loden pockets, watching the house for signs.

"Smell," the father says.

"I'm cold," the daughter says. "I can see my breath."

"That's impossible. Look at these reds," the father says. "Elm leaves maybe. Maple."

"I have a burr in my shoe," the daughter says.

The father jiggers the leaves with a length of branch, scaring up cindery flecks. "You're sounding just like her," the father says. "Really. You know what that's liable to spell?"

"No, I don't," the daughter says.

"Then too bad for you," the father says.

The mother is lying in bed smoking filterless cigarettes filched from the father's jacket pocket. A windfall of linens—wash towels, kerchiefs, lingerie—is scattered around her, wrung out, reused. She has twist-top bottles the color of some kind of syrup in bed with her, too, and same-colored stains of it, a few spoons needing washing, a mateless sock, a thermometer—which does not work—a butane lighter, a wristwatch—scratched—pumpkin seeds, makeup, crusts of toast.

"Tell me," the mother says to the daughter, who stands by her bedside. "What time is it? What were you all that time up to together back out there?"

"Just upkeep is all," the daughter says.

"Save it," the mother says. "Hand me that lipstick."

"Where?" the daughter says.

The mother blows a smoke ring. "Make a wish," she says. "Some color becomes me, your father said. Once."

"It would," the daughter says. "Now."

"If what?" the mother says.

"Beats me," the daughter says. "Anyway, suppertime's coming up soon."

"Again?" the mother says.

Nothing is out in the yard except for what rightly, by nature, belongs there. The usual stirrings—flappings, flickering things. A slight shudder of brier. A rumor of frost. Tall grasses and weedy things. Garden and yard tools dirtied with earth. There are scootings and squirrelings. Whiffings. Hoots. Cool acorns, pinecones, thistle and fluff. Things that drift down slowly, softly. Scratchings. Markings. Tender signs—if one is looking to see them.

"He says to stop raiding his pockets," the daughter says to the mother, who taps an ash off on the wadded bedding by way of response. "Do you know what you're doing is asking for trouble?"

"I know what I know," the mother says.

The daughter turns and looks out the bedroom window.

"Do you?" the mother says.

"Couldn't you pick this place up?" the daughter says.

"What kind of an answer is that?" the mother says.

The daughter says to the father, "It's raining—and that's not the half of it, either."

The daughter believes that the father often enters her room at times when she is not there, and that he opens her dresser drawers. She images the father handling fabric, possibly running a finger the delicate length of a seam.

She is of the impression that sooner or later the father

slips himself into her bed, but not to rest. Instead, she envisions the father regarding the ceiling above his head, maybe taking note of the slightest beginnings of water damage there.

The daughter can never seem to sleep in her bed at night. Night after night, she lies alert, aware of the bedclothes touching her skin. Looking up, in the light of the moon coming in through the parted window lace, what the daughter sees on the ceiling is next to nothing.

The father has followed the daughter into the kitchen, where she is setting the kettle down on the range flame.
"There's work needs doing outside," the father says.
"Maybe later," the daughter says.
"When?" the father says.
The daughter yawns. "Search me," she says. "I'm all the time so sleepy."
"Tea is the ticket," the father says.
"I wonder," the daughter says, "why would a person talk in their sleep."
"Plenty of sugar," the father says. "And milk."
The daughter opens a carton and sniffs. "God, is this evil," she says.
"Who do you know who talks in their sleep?" the father says, shutting the flame off.
"Nobody," the daughter says. "That's who."

The daughter has fallen asleep in the mother's bed, with her arms around the mother, and with most of the mother's soiled belongings pushed over to one side.

The daughter is out behind the house, in the place where the ground is scarred. The air is crisp and still, and there is just the slightest motion of a curtain as the daughter tends to burning what she is burning one by one. **Q**

DAWN RAFFEL

Inland

Ribbons? The sisters have them. Plenty. A collection. "Keepers" on assorted spools, in loops, in rolls, in cello wraps, in stages of unravelment—grosgrains, velveteens, moirés, finger widths of satins oh so smooth and only slightly soiled, tatted laces laid in strips alongside the sisters' bureau glasses, sewn brocades, paper ribbons made for curling on a scissor's split, souvenirs in jewel hues the sisters have the names to: ruby, amber, amethyst, carnelian, tourmaline, and still the blues, the *cordons bleu,* the turquoises, the sapphires, ribbons to go with the shoes that were dyed to match the matching evening gowns they never wore themselves but once, stiffened bows with plastic diamond fasteners, Swiss-dot samples, clinquant snippets, sequined bits the sisters decked the long-gone poodle's ears with, streamers unstrung from the neighbor's wreaths, sashes that cinched the waists of the sisters' nieces once removed, locket braidings, bobbin threadings, golden bands that held the sisters' coifs on high occasions and that hold, the sisters like to think, a certain scent of ladyfingers, finger-dusted strands, still.

Picture the boxes.

Picture breath.

Picture one of the sisters asking the other to hold the skein. Handy bounty. Afternoons of kitty's cradle, casting off, croquet, or, as the other sister might insist, crochet; twilight times apprising one another on the filigrees and appliqués, the true-to-life rosettes, the helix stencils, tying up their time with taking tea with one another, but still not, they wish to think, the least like one another. One trims, the other draws the line.

Also, in the second place, not both of them make braided cakes with cardamom, steep foxglove in infusions for the heart. Pedigree means nothing much to one of them, *mal de mer* means something to the other. For company, for family, one tinkles on the spinet and the other washes saucers. One is older, which is something one of them will not forget. One, according to the other, has a bee stuck in her bonnet. Both are keepers, packers-in. Nights, the sisters comb and brush and floss and bless and flush, and flutter at the Levelors and pull the curtains' cording tight.

Picture what is missing from inside the sisters' lockets.

Foxgloves are the base for digitalis. They are amethyst in tone. To keep them, one must keep them dry.

Keep, for keeps, keep at it, persevere, keep company, keep up, keep faith with, pray the Lord one's soul to keep, keep from, housekeep, nourish, keep one's head on, take a little keepsake, prevent one's feathers becoming ruffled, keep one's colors true and blue, keep the happy home fires burning, keep the cards and letters coming, keep the pots all boiling, persevere, have starch and honor, decorate, try *fleurs-de-lis*, keep going even on a shoestring, turn a cheek and stiffen a lip, maintain, support, prevent, and be one's sister's keeper, keep on ticking tape, keep spinning yarns, keep kicking up the ante, keep on offering it up, slide up on it by inches and by doses, maintain etiquette, try gossamers, try tourniquets and tendrils. Take a powder. Hold one's breath. Keep the fibrillations quiet. Let the kitten take one's tongue. Let sleeping dogs lie. Keep the peace.

Picture a loop, a hole, a snap.

Capisce? Q

DAWN RAFFEL

The Pleiades

Shhhh . . . In here, over here, do you see us? See us, chiffoned and lushy and luxe for the shindy which Mother has planned? See us lifting our finger wave, follow-me-lads off-ear and aloft so that Mother will touch us with *eau*? Oh, fluid ambrosia! Brush us splendid! Do us the dewiest rush! "Sugar-cups," Mother is saying, "please to hold *still*!" The silly! Impossible! Us? Hold still, sit tight, with our family dog, our family Labby, wagging and whuffing and kissing knee, and us fluffed up in our laciest scanties and petties, too? Oh, we simply must wiggle so much! Must sniff at each other's glossed aroma . . . flowerish, potion-y, womanish, posh . . . "Goodness," Mother is saying, "shoo him away! That beast of a Blackie, shoo him away!" *Woof!* Poor fellow! Snufflish, antsy-ish, glintsy boy. Boy! And us, just fancy, whirling for Mother around, a-ribbon and puckered, ticklish us—see?—aflow in Mother's vanny glass and overrim of shiny gild, fleeciest lassies, downiest finery-feathered height! Top of the toe! Oh, rosy floatatiousness! Swishle of pinafore! Lilt! and flutter, the flutter of fingertips, Mother's, nimble as Jill's, liquidy quick. *"Perfect,"* Mother is saying, and something-ensembles . . . "so cautious . . . precious . . . social reception" . . . on and on, and oh, such pooched and plumed exhalings are warming our shinnies and . . . "Lambikins, are you minding me?" Mother! "Of course . . . lovely . . . exquisite . . . pinkies, elbows . . . very polite . . . listen to me, are you listening?" Us? Us, with the music of newness lapping our ears, all seashell song, all beckoning whoosh? . . . "And courteous . . . curtsy . . ." *Feel! Just feel*! . . . "Oh, this irascible menace on paws, what in the world shall we do?" Do? On our honor, what to do but brilly off to the floral-leaf garden? Buttercups! Marigolds! Mother's relations sheathed in frou-frou, gents in belly-band elegance, all.

Oh, whites and crease-y britches, sleeves! Oh, buttonhole-tuckers and coattailed afts. Ruffle and fringe! The French corsages, tipsy fingers—don't you see the wisp-bouquets? The upsy-daisied, underwreaths of rolled chignons? Slipknots here! and bow ties nestled next to gleaming points pressed smooth . . . oooh . . . Smoothest us, tidiest us, airily offering Mother's confections, silvered servers, pouring glam. "Fetching darlings . . . luscious . . . stepping so prettily" . . . Hear? Do you hear? Such chatter regarding us *demoiselles*! The sweets! Please, partake of our tasty delicacies, sipple summer's salty dainties, smell. Inhale! Oh, suckle of honey! Oh, missies! Oh, whiskerish bliss; oh, trickle of peepers and trellised lash; oh, willied sigh and wave on furrow, drizzled punch and goldenrod and linen-doilied, folded scents! Oh, nosies gay and mumsy drops and little lambsied, ivory us! Sunny us over, ladle us, ray us, la so fa ti do, ringing our ringlets in light. Belles and beaux to share and share us! Show us your fastening purses, sashes, usher us close to tuckle your streamers, link your cuffs! See us chiffondled? Tousle our locks! Let us smooch your cheeks, your chins, your lacy, unseen breath; let us see us darkly pooled in shoes, in woozy polish, plummish luster . . . "Ready, sugars, sugarplums?" Oh, it is Mother! Mother, Mother blossom-toned. Father! piping up and up, the world, the world, to pie-eye us, our dance—see us, spin and spin alike, a-lit to scale to nectar-reaches, *tour jeté en pointes* as glissed as wings, as quivered arches in the ribboned heat, oh heat, oh height and land a-spindle under us and dizzy, dizzy over us is swoony blueing, heatening white, our tremble-curtsies streaking, clap of fingers, clap of palms, of heart, of heart, of roarish ocean, deafening, a tidal lip, a scream, a shriek we cannot stop—"Please, oh please, you must, must, must let him out, the dog, the dog, oh *please*!" Q

LILY TUCK

Every Time I Have a Cup of This Tea, I Will Think of Africa

Even the sound of her own voice, Frances tells George and Bibi, George's brand-new wife and Frances's brand-new sister-in-law—even the sound of her own voice sounds much too large to her in Africa. Everything is so darn large in Africa. Even the minibus they are driving in with the driver that George has hired for them from the hotel in Nairobi, even it seems to Frances too large for just a minibus. Anyway, what matters, of course, is that the minibus gets them there safely and back, to and from the game park.

Oh, but the elephants, too, make a big impression on Frances! And Frances is the first one to admit this, she says, and Frances is speaking now of the elephant the time when the minibus was coming around the bend, and right in front of them, blocking the minibus, was not just an elephant but an elephant with a baby, no less! Well, George had told the driver to just go ahead and honk the horn—but, of course, George was only kidding, he told Frances later. Anyway, the mother elephant raised up her trunk at them and her ears were flapping like crazy, which is what Frances says she will never forget—the big noise the mother elephant's ears made. Frances says she cannot even begin to describe this gigantic flapping noise. Just like on a sailboat, the noise wet canvas makes in a sudden squall in Maine, where Frances, as a young girl, and before she started to work at the bank, used to spend her summers. The same kind of noise, Frances says. Terrifying, she says.

All this, however, happens before they have to get in the rickety-looking plane to visit Bibi's brother—Christopher.

Chris.

Well, the plane is as hot as an oven—my God, as a microwave oven! Frances tells Bibi, and every few minutes, George, who sits across the aisle from them, takes out a large white pocket handkerchief and wipes his face, his neck. God, the plane smells! It smells, Frances thinks, of that special African smell, a sour, orangy, fruit smell.

The pilot has announced that the flight from Nairobi is a two-hour flight. He has repeated—Frances assumes—the same information to them in Swahili. Most of the pilots here, George says to reassure Frances and Bibi, are British. The others are French. Or Italian. The plane is an Otter. An Otter can land anywhere, George says. An Otter can land in a ditch if need be.

Frances says, "How do you know? You're not a pilot."

Frances is older than George, and George, Frances knows—although he has not said by how much exactly—is a good deal older than Bibi. Bibi, Frances guesses, is thirty-two or thirty-three—thirty-five years old at the most.

Frances looks out the window. They are flying over the Rift Valley, and again Frances is tempted to say something about the size of things—about the clouds. Instead, she says, "Christopher—I mean, Chris, your brother—will be there, won't he? Chris, you said, would meet us, Bibi."

Bibi says, "Before Kenya, Chris spent two years in Costa Rica. Chris said Costa Rica was completely different. You'll see," Bibi says. "I mean, you would never know that we were twins. Or, for that matter, brother and sister. Related even."

Frances shuts her eyes. She tries to picture Chris, picture how he looks, picture where he lives. Just before the plane touches down, she says, "What is your real name, anyhow, Bibi? I've been meaning to ask. Bibi stands for what?"

Bibi calls across the aisle, "Look—oh, I see him! Over there by the jeep—the green jeep! I'm sure that's him! Chris! George. I can see him from the window! See Chris!"

"Outside? See Chris where, Bibi?" George says.

"I guess I'm just excited," Bibi says.

. . .

Inside the air terminal, Frances looks at the people waiting outside the gate—at the white people. She hears Bibi give a little cry, and with her passport held high in the air, Bibi has started to run. Frances sees a young man in a light cotton suit. The young man is blond, and Frances, too, starts to wave to him.

"Chris!"

Chris has on running shorts and a T-shirt that says Lomotil on it. He wears flip-flop rubber sandals. His hair is light brown, darker than Bibi's. Past Chris, past Bibi, and past George, who is shaking Chris's hand up and down, Frances looks for the young man in the light cotton suit—but the blond young man is gone.

On the way to the school in the Land Rover, Bibi is talking to Chris—filling him in, Bibi says. Frances has never seen Bibi look so animated, so young. But Bibi *is* young, Frances reminds herself, although she has no need to. Next to her, in the back of the Land Rover, George, Frances thinks, has picked up that sour, orangy, African smell—the smell Frances can never quite name and say what it smells of—and George, as if he could read Frances's mind, says, "It's a lot hotter here, wouldn't you say, Frances? Hotter than Nairobi, I mean. But it's not just the heat, it's the whole atmosphere. I can feel it—it's different."

"It's poorer," Frances says. "It's poorer here, right, Chris?"

Bibi is telling Chris about someone who left a really obscene message on someone else's answering machine, only someone else—a third person whose name Frances does not catch, a name that sounds like Attila—by mistake listened to the message first.

"What did you say, Frances?" Chris is still laughing. "I can't hear you! You have to shout! The road! The roads are terrible! You should see after the rains! Solid mud! No traction, not even in four-wheel drive!"

"It doesn't matter!" Frances yells back.

Frances looks out the window at houses—little huts—and at women squatting and washing. On the side of the road there are children tending goats. The goats are black and white, and a few of them are standing straight up on their hind legs in order to tear the leaves off the trees. The goats remind Frances of laundry left out to dry. Frances sighs to herself. She is suddenly feeling tired.

Chris is telling Bibi about the car, about the Land Rover. Chris says he bought the Land Rover secondhand. From a Brit. The Brit, Chris says, had to leave. The Brit got sick. So sick his urine turned brown. Black almost, Chris tells Bibi.

"Yuck," Bibi says.

"At first, he thought it was just hepatitis, but what was I saying?" Chris says. "Oh—the Land Rover's engine is completely rebuilt, though you'd never know from the sound of it. The Brit also put in a spare gas tank. Right underneath where you're sitting, Bibi. Full, the Land Rover can hold two hundred liters. But spare parts are a bitch. I almost wrote you to bring me two of everything." Chris laughs. "We're nearly there," he says. "You guys back there must be tired."

George says, "No. Hot."

Chris says, "Costa Rica was hotter, but not as humid as here. The humidity makes a big difference."

"The first car I ever owned," George says, leaning toward the front of the Land Rover, "was a Studebaker. Remember the Studebaker? No, you're too young. It was designed by Raymond Loewy. I was in college then. I swear to God, I spent more time underneath the hood of that Studebaker than in class or studying."

"Here. Here we are, folks," Chris says. "Welcome to my village."

"*Hola,*" Bibi says.

Frances sees a row of houses. Small stores. Over one of the houses, she can still make out the sign: BARCLAY'S BANK.

"Frances—you see that?" George nudges her. "Have you told Chris yet how you've come to open a new branch?"

Three women are selling fruit. As the car turns off the road, one of the women jumps to her feet. She shouts out at them. "Hello! Hello, American!"

In answer, Chris honks the horn of the Land Rover; he waves his hand.

"*Hola,*" Bibi says again. She, too, waves at the woman.

"See?" Chris looks back at Frances. "See the field? We're going to plant corn in there. That's also part of the program. Before that there was nothing. In between the rows, they can plant something else. Potatoes, vegetables."

"That's what we did in Connecticut," George says. "We broke up the vegetable rows with flowers—nasturtiums and what's the other kind called? Marigolds? That's what we always used to do."

There is a silence. Then Bibi says, "I told George right away. I said, George, I don't have a green thumb—absolutely not. Some people don't."

Chris says, "There's my house. Over there. See it? The one built over the waterfall."

Frances laughs.

They are walking across the wet grass to the school and Chris is telling Frances how difficult it is to try to teach in Africa. Chris teaches math. Chris also says he teaches Current Events. Current events, Chris tells Frances, is his idea and not a part of the official school curriculum.

A boy of thirteen or so wearing short khaki shorts comes up to them.

Bibi says, "Boy, look at his legs. Legs at least a mile long. Who was it—remember, George—who ran that marathon?

Ran barefoot and won? He was an African fellow, wasn't he?"

"A goatherd from Ethiopia," George answers. "I don't remember his name."

Frances says, "You run, don't you? You run in Stamford, Bibi?"

Bibi says, "Hey, young fellow, what's your name? You don't mind if I take your picture, do you?"

"Jimmy Thiongo," the boy says.

Bibi says, "Here. Here, Jimmy, write down your name for me. Your name and your address. I promise to send you the picture."

Chris opens the door to a classroom—a low dark rectangular room filled helter-skelter with metal desks and crooked chairs; a still unerased blackboard with equations on it stands against the far wall.

"E equals MC squared," George says.

Chris says, "The way you can tell this is also the science lab is the science lab has a sink and a Bunsen burner that doesn't work in it. Most of the kids don't own pencils or paper. It's midterm, you know, so they've gone home now. They're supposed to go home and bring back their tuition. Needless to say, a lot of them do not come back. Not ever," Chris says.

"How much is the tuition?—in dollars," George asks.

"What about him?" Frances says. "Jimmy Thiongo. Why doesn't Jimmy Thiongo go home?"

Jimmy Thiongo has been following them. Frances turns around and smiles at him.

Chris shares his house with a teacher, a teacher named Kale. Kale has gone home to his village for the midterm break, and Frances, Chris says, is to sleep in Kale's bedroom, in Kale's bed.

Frances looks around Kale's bedroom. She sees a small bureau, a chair, a calendar that hangs on the wall. She also sees a light bulb that has been filled with earth and fashioned into a flower pot. Behind her, Chris stands in the doorway and surveys the room as if for the first time.

"I promised Kale I would water the ivy while he was away," Chris says.

"Oh, the ivy in the light bulb, you mean," Frances says. "I thought the ivy wasn't real, I thought the leaves were plastic."

Chris says, "Someone gave the plant to Kale. The cutting came all the way from—from I forget where—the States somewhere. It was a joke. The plant with the Harvard education is what Kale calls it."

"Oh, I get it," Frances says. "Ivy. Ivy League."

The other thing Frances notices about Kale's room is that it has the smell in it, the sour, orangy, African smell—the walls, the bureau, the chair, the bed, the ivy plant, too, probably. How can she sleep with such a smell? She cannot. She does not sleep at all. In the morning, she says, "You know the kind of night you feel you didn't sleep a wink, you didn't shut your eyes once? I kept looking at my watch—one o'clock, two o'clock, three, four—the luminous dial. Also, I kept thinking about Kale. About what if he comes back all of a sudden."

"Don't you wish," Bibi says.

"No." Frances blushes. "No, that's not what I mean, Bibi," Frances says.

When Bibi, Chris, George, and Frances are getting ready to leave the house to go sightseeing, they see Jimmy Thiongo standing next to the Land Rover.

George says, "What does he want? Is he trying to sell us drugs, or what?"

Bibi says, "This reminds me of when I was in Thailand that time I told you about, George."

Jimmy Thiongo says, "You did not give me your address—

your address in America. You," says Jimmy Thiongo, pointing his finger at Frances.

"Oh no, you mean Bibi—Bibi, my sister-in-law. Bibi," Frances calls out, "the boy wants *your* address. Bibi, Jimmy Thiongo wants your address in Stamford, Connecticut."

All morning Chris drives George, Bibi, and Frances in the Land Rover. They visit a coffee plantation. They visit a tea plantation. They stop at an outdoor market, where Bibi buys some cloth that she says she will wear as a sarong this summer or, if she and George go to the Caribbean, this winter. Frances is tempted to buy some cloth as well, but she does not want to appear to be copying Bibi. In the end, Frances buys a small bag of tea.

"Every time I have a cup of this tea, I will think of Africa," Frances starts to say. But no one is listening. George, who is examining Bibi's cloth, says, "Probably made in Taiwan."

Bibi tells Chris she is so hungry she could eat an elephant, and Chris takes them to the Sheraton Hotel. In the bar, they order beers and Chris runs into a couple he knows. The man, whose name is Alois and who is Swiss, tells them a joke. About Africans. His wife says that the joke is not funny and that she has heard it before anyway about Poles. Still, everyone laughs. So does Frances. She is tired from bouncing up and down on the back seat of the Land Rover, and the Sheraton Hotel bar is air-conditioned.

"It's the beer," Frances says to Alois's wife and to no one in particular. She also says, "But funny you should mention a light bulb in your joke. In my room—well, no, the room I am sleeping in—the room really belongs to another teacher, a friend of Chris, only he's away, a young man named Kale—isn't that right, Chris? Anyhow, what this reminded me of was that he—the teacher, Kale—has a light bulb in his room—no, no, I mean the light bulb has ivy growing out of it. Isn't this strange? Or is this an African custom?" Frances says.

Again Frances is awake all night. She is in the bathroom. Something she ate. The pills Frances has brought along with her are of no use at all. In the morning, Frances refuses to eat. Only tea, she says. Frances sips a little tea for breakfast, and she says that she will not be going to Lake Boringo with them, after all.

Chris says, "We could postpone it, Frances. Go tomorrow."

George says, "Chris says Lake Boringo is full of crocodiles. Hippos, too. If we don't come back, Frances, please tell the kids one of them has to take the dog—Hannibal."

"The thing is not to fall in the water," Bibi says. "Like in Cannes, there is this boat that takes you parachuting over all these yachts. Big yachts. Expensive yachts. Yachts that belong to people like the King of Morocco."

When Frances hears the Land Rover leave, she goes back to bed. She feels better. Actually, she quite likes how empty her stomach feels, how her hip bones jut out. She reminds herself of those Indians—Indian Indians—who can levitate and who can take out their intestines in order to wash them—wash them in the Ganges River, Frances imagines. Just before Frances falls asleep, she notices the guidebook on the floor. She should have given the guidebook to Bibi, to take along with them, Frances thinks. Or to George. Lake Boringo, the guidebook says, is a birdwatcher's paradise.

Frances knows when she wakes up that it must be about noon. The light. The heat. The silence broken only by the mating buzz of two flies over by the windowsill. Frances looks up at Kale's ivy. If Chris had not told her, she would have sworn the ivy was plastic. The light-bulb arrangement makes Frances think of Maine again—the house where she used to spend her summers. There, too, light bulbs hung from the walls—only those light bulbs were filled with a liquid—a liquid to extinguish a fire. The theory was that the glass would break when it got too hot.

Frances sits outside on Chris's small porch. She is drinking tea and reading. When she looks up, Jimmy Thiongo is there in front of her. He is standing on one long leg; one foot is resting on the other.

"They have gone to Lake Boringo. They should be back in a little while," Frances says.

"Lake Boringo," Jimmy Thiongo says.

"Have you been to Lake Boringo? It is a two-hour drive—at least. That's what Chris said," Frances says.

Jimmy Thiongo shakes his head.

"Lots of birds there," Frances says. "Lots of flamingos."

"Flamingos," Jimmy Thiongo says.

"I was sick. Something I ate. I feel a lot better. Look here." Frances hands Jimmy Thiongo the guidebook, which she has opened to the Lake Boringo section.

Jimmy Thiongo takes the book from Frances and glances at it. He shrugs and hands it back. Frances thinks that perhaps Jimmy Thiongo does not know how to read.

"You want to show me something?" Jimmy Thiongo says.

"What? Show you what?"

Jimmy Thiongo shrugs. "Your camera. Show me your camera," he says.

"Oh, but it's Bibi's camera. I don't own a camera. I don't like to take pictures," Frances says. "I prefer to look. If you have a camera, you're never really looking, are you? You're always looking at things in terms of a picture, if you see what I mean."

"One day I am wanting a camera," Jimmy Thiongo says.

"Bibi is Chris's sister. Is Chris your teacher?" Frances says.

Jimmy Thiongo says, "I saw some people, and they were having the kind of camera where the picture comes out straightaway. I don't want to be having that kind of camera. I want to be having a real camera."

"I don't know what kind of camera Bibi has," Frances says. "But I'm sure it's a good camera. I can ask her if you like. Bibi is married to my brother, George. Excuse me for a minute," Frances says.

She has felt something move in her stomach.

When Frances returns to the porch, both the boy and the guidebook are gone.

Frances does not mention the guidebook. But Bibi mentions her camera—a Pentax that has been stolen, Bibi says. "Where we had lunch," Bibi says. "Oh, Frances, you should have seen it right in the middle of the lake—Lake Boringo—an island, with these little tents everywhere. You would have loved the tents, Frances. Tents with dressing tables and luggage racks inside them. Straight out of—what do you call her?—Karen Blixen."

"Isak Dinesen," Frances says.

"Yes. That's what it was like where we had lunch," Bibi says. "Buffet-style, and with all these different kinds of salads. We haven't had any salad since we've been in Africa. Because the salad in the hotel in Nairobi does not count. You can't count a salad like that. Anyhow—the camera was hanging by the strap from the back of my chair and someone must have taken it while I was helping myself at the buffet. I went twice, I remember. Coffee and dessert, they brought to the table," Bibi says. "Isn't that right, George? You ate dessert. A waiter, maybe. Who else was there? I mean, who else was there who could have taken the camera? There were these two English girls. You should have seen them, Frances—they went *water-skiing*. Crazy. And speaking of not offending anyone, they were wearing bikinis. Oh, George, admit it," Bibi says, "those girls were crazy. Whereas why bother to wear anything at all, is what I say," Bibi says.

"What about the crocodiles?" Frances says. "And the hippopotamuses, did you see any?"

"George says we are insured," Bibi says, "but what I really mind losing is not the camera so much as the pictures I took. Pictures of—oh—what was the name of that boy, George? And the elephant, too—remember, Frances? The big mother elephant with the baby that was blocking the minibus in the game park. I just know I got a good picture of her. Oh, and Frances? Frances, are you feeling all right?"

This time Frances sits in the front of the Land Rover next to Chris, who is driving. She feels fine, right as rain, Frances has assured everyone—only she is still a little anxious. For instance, what if she has to ask Chris to stop for her somewhere on their way to Aberdare and in the middle of nowhere? As a precaution, Frances has stuffed her pockets with pink toilet paper.

"It's just luck!" Chris shouts to Frances over the roar of the engine noise. "A friend of mine who spent two years out here, nothing ever happened to him! He was never robbed is what I am saying! But first thing you know, when he goes back to the States and he's making a phone call—he's calling home actually—he turns around and his backpack is gone! Everything he owned was in that backpack! His passport, his clothes, his diary! He kept a diary! A journal! Makes you sick, doesn't it, Frances, when you hear stories like this!"

"Where I work, I'm always hearing about people losing things—how they lose their money!" Frances says.

"No, no!" Chris says. "There's no way I can make money here in Africa!"

On the way, they have trouble with the Land Rover. The engine won't turn over.

Chris says, "A vapor lock. This has happened before."

George says, "To me it sounds more like the battery."

Frances says that she knows nothing about cars and that she is not going to say a word.

Anyway, when they get going again, the paved road is full of potholes, and in the back Bibi says that she does not have enough meat on her bones to ride like this. Frances offers to trade places and move into the seat next to George—but George says for Frances to stay put and that Bibi is always exaggerating and that Chris had better just keep going if they are ever going to get to the Aberdare Golf Club. George also says, "I can already taste it—Tanqueray with a twist."

Bibi says, "I don't always exaggerate, George. You exaggerate, George. You exaggerated about how different everything was going to be here. But it isn't! Africans are people, too, you know! I'm going to have a Campari-and-soda! Either a Campari-and-soda or a Bloody Mary!" Bibi yells.

"On a clear day you can see Mount Kenya from Aberdare, only it's going to be dark when we get there!" Chris shouts.

Frances shouts, "The boy—Jimmy Thiongo—who was hanging around the house all the time—Chris, is he a good student?"

Yesterday, Today, and Tomorrow, Frances will always remember, was what was written on the tag—the little white tag attached to the flower bush. To Frances, the flowers looked like impatiens. But at the Aberdare Golf Club, all the flower bushes had African names. Mary would have known. Mary would have known if they were the same. Mary loved to garden. Mary—George's first wife—about whom no one ever speaks. Well, Frances did not speak of her, either. Frances did not want to spoil things. Frances wanted to be fair. Otherwise, when George had asked her if she wanted to come along with them on this trip, shouldn't she have said no?

"Maybe I could do something for that Thiongo boy!" Frances shouts. "Maybe I could pay for his tuition! Until he has finished this term, anyway! I could be—you know, like his fairy godmother!"

"Oh. Oh, Frances, no, no, no!" Chris shouts. "You don't know what you'd be getting into! You don't know what you'd be getting involved in!"

"Involved in what?" Bibi yells from the back. "Who are you two talking about, Chris?"

"Jimmy Thiongo!" Chris yells. "The boy you took the picture of, Bibi! I was just telling Frances that he is one of the boys who can't pay his tuition!"

"I still have his address!" Bibi screams. "Oh, if only I knew who stole my camera!" Bibi screams.

"You see, I have this idea," Frances will say much later when she is back home at a certain type of party and maybe when she has had one drink too many. Her idea—and it will make all the difference, Frances will say—is to move—literally move it all, move it lock, stock, and barrel, move everything, the dorms, the libraries, the books, the professors, the whole kit and caboodle to Africa. First Harvard and then Yale. Then maybe Princeton, too, even. Frances will say she means it, and after all, she doesn't care what anyone else thinks. Besides, she will say she thinks everyone here is an idiot, anyway. Frances will say, "Someone moved the Cloisters to Manhattan all the way from Italy, you know. Or from France, or Spain."

Another thing that Frances will always remember is how, during dinner that night in Aberdare, Bibi said that her mother did not know that she was going to have twins.

"Honest. She didn't have a clue," Bibi said. "And the doctor didn't, either. I mean, the doctor was packing up his stuff—his instruments and things—when all of a sudden he goes, 'Oops, wait a minute, here comes another one.'"

"You or Chris, Bibi?" Frances will remember herself saying. "Who is older?"

And, of course, strawberries—Frances will remember that for dessert they ate strawberries. They were the small, sweet, French kind—*fraises des bois.* **Q**

LISA WOHL

Kalighat

    After we took the train—
  After the driver pedaled us there—
  After we saw the goat cut—
  After we saw blood rush out onto the stone—
  After we walked to the room—
  After I soaked in the old—it looked to me then like a tub with hooves—
  After he poured the hot tea from the chipped pot into the chipped cups—
  After he lifted up the netting that kept the flies from the milk—
  After he put his spoon into my tea—
  After I went away from him to the far end of the room—
  After I saw that there were boys who sat there at the far end of the room—
  After I saw the boys draw on ropes to move the mats—
  After I saw the mats move—
  After he said for me not to mind, that the boys had seen it all—
  After he made me lie down—
  After I said, No, no, let's do it standing up—
  After I heard the falling of the mats—
  After I took him with me to the tub—
  After we stood on the stone—
  After I took his hand and kneeled on my knees—
  After I took him in my mouth—
  After he said for me never to mind the boys—
  After everything that covered me fell—
  After I looked and saw the boys look—

After he looked—
After the water fell—
After I heard the mats—
After I saw the goat—
After I died—
Then I died and died again.

"The Kali Temple at Kalighat near a small canal called Adigunga (the real "Ganga" because it is thought to be the original bed of the Hoogly) does not allow foreigners to enter. Built in 1809, the Kali is one of Hinduism's best-known pilgrimage sites, containing shrines to Radha, Shiva, Khrishna, and Kali. Human sacrifices were claimed to have been made in the last century, but only goats are done away with now."
Witherspoon's India Including Nepal
Completely Revised and Updated

Ride it. Full bore, open, rush—train, train, train. **Q**

LISA WOHL

Wafer

I was nibbling on her knuckles. Then I sucked on her toes. I said I just had to take a big bite of her cheek. "That's silly," she said. "Who ever heard of a person eating a person?" She was too young to tell about cannibals. Or about mothers. Too young to tell about fathers, how I eat her father, how her father eats me, our Holy Communion, and that there is worship in it. Still, I could see why she put her hand over her cheek.

"People eat things," she said.

"Oranges, pizza, hot dogs, and . . . *ears!*" I said.

Her hands moved to hide her ears.

"I can't help myself," I said. I took little nibbling nips of her neck and saw her cheeks go red.

"Stop!" she said.

She twisted her head around, but then she turned to me and I felt her breath on my face. She went for my mouth. She was kissing and chewing my mouth. She kept on kissing and pressing in hard on my mouth—until my lip got cut somehow.

She was too young for me to say what I wanted to say, so I said, "Let's do something. I know, let's make a cake."

"I know," she said, "we can make a cake."

We got out the butter, the sugar, the flour, the vanilla, the baking powder, the eggs, the salt. She cut the butter into lumps, oiling her fingers with each lump.

I dipped my finger into the bowl and licked my finger. She dipped her finger in the bowl and licked her finger.

"Mmmmmmm," she said.

"Mmmmmmm," I said.

It was sickening. The taste was the taste that fills your mouth—all the people, not just her, in your mouth. **Q**

DIANE WILLIAMS

Pussy

The woman's knowledge gives her vicious pleasure. She could have understood sooner if she had only tried to understand. Now that she understands, she will just not leave the men alone, now that she understands that everything that matters has nothing to do with her expectation of loyalty and devotion from a person she is hoping is nearly perfect. Oh yes, now the woman is full of desire as she climbs the stairs to her room. The stairs glow for her eyes. The woman sees a man heads taller than she is jump out at her and then turn back away. He is subtracting things from himself, because she can see only his trouser leg and his one shoe as he goes into her room.

Upon her entering her room after him, the woman does something significant and full of meaning.

Albeit, the orange orange, the thin, dry, oval slice of gray bread—oh no, there was even something more concealed in some silver foil—the elixir the woman knows emanates from these hors d'oeuvres which are all hers, on her tray, on the table, at the end of her bed—amounts to what the woman is if I say so. She equals anything at all on my say-so. The woman is a little dirty thrill.

This is the haunting story of a young man who married for love and who found himself in the grip of a considerable poonac. **Q**

DIANE WILLIAMS

The Care of Myself

So why can't everything be perfect? God love him, he appealed to me. He had startled me into feeling an incredible amount of affection for a stranger—him. Still, I could have made mad passionate love to him, this inspector who rang my doorbell, who had dressed himself as a fireman.

"Do you have a wound? Is that a bandage on your head?" I asked him.

He tugged on the stretchy cloth which was not supposed to be hidden under his helmet. He said, "We all wear that."

The days and the years pass so swiftly.

Now, what I am doing for my wound is this: I stick any old rag or balled-up old sock I can find as close to it as I can get. Belly-down on the floor, with my reading glasses on, I've also got some filler sticking almost into my asshole. With my bawdy book here to comfort me right in front of my nose—we are both, the book and I, products of a great civilization—I take the plunge. I am thrusting mightily, and sometimes I manage to get hurt again. **Q**

DIANE WILLIAMS

Clean

This begins where so many others have ended, where the man and his wife are going to live the rest of their entire lives in perfect joy, so they arrive at the train station.

Now we're on our way. I'm dooteedooteedoing as if I'm happy. Went to the mail where I go to get it. Touched it. Washed myself. Meticulously washed out my contraceptive device with Cascade or Joy.

I toasted a piece of toast for myself to eat, buttered it, put cheese on it, drank coffee I had made, orange juice I had squeezed, took care of the other people. Put away food. I washed. I washed. I never thought I'd get the semen off my ring. The speed of my thought was a deep offense to me. It should have taken me a lifetime to find out how not to be happy just to ensure perfect success. **Q**

DIANE WILLIAMS

Ore

A generally reliable woman was pestering the seed—or is it called a pit?—that she had noticed was blotchy. The reliable woman at work in her kitchen observed privately to herself, for no reason she knew of, that the pit had been discolored by avocado-colored markings. The woman was using her fingers to wrench the pit out from the center of the ripe fruit. The pit was not coming along willingly.

No, this is not about childbirth.

The surprise is that anyone as reliable as she is had not had plenty of experience wrenching pits.

The pear's pit—this is an avocado pear pit—was not of a like mind to hers—like, *What is the matter with you, pit?*

What is the matter with her very reliable husband, who could not extract this woman, his wife, from their home?

The wife had been making her husband miserable for years, being the unbudgeable type.

I'd say time for a change.

In their secret life, the husband and the wife then sought the usual marital excavations—their aim being to meet their troubles with equanimity.

For starters, they agreed. They agreed how excellent their sexual satisfactions together were, how much more reliably attainable these satisfactions were, more now than had ever been the case before, now that every other aspect of their life together, they admitted, was so unsatisfactory in such extreme.

No, no, no, no, no!

This discussion never occurred. The husband and the wife no longer had the means to conduct such a high-level discussion.

These people are annoying. You know how annoying? To me, as annoying as it was to see for myself last night at twilight one bright sparkling spot in the sky that did not move. It did not get bigger, or brighter, or smaller, or dimmer, and for all intents and purposes, it is stuck there.

As I am. **Q**

DIANE WILLIAMS

Seraphim

I suppose that I do have places, a few places, left to wear my mustache to. I have worn it almost everywhere. Before we go, I put on my fur coat inside of my house simultaneous with my putting it on. My mustache is faint and spiky. My coat is thick and dark.

Going around town tends to be sad, like walking around behind a dog who won't go. You wear what you wear. Tonight we are going to the Fontana for pizza. There will be a TV on in there. There will be plastic chandeliers to simulate glass chandeliers. There will be simulated oil paintings on the wall to simulate the idea of things: a woman with a hat on, perhaps her skirt roughed up by the wind, her hand lifted to keep her bonnet on her head.

When the pizza comes, I put a fingertip into my plate to get a crumb stuck to it, then to lick the crumb off.

This is my gift to my children—whereas theirs to me is not to be nasty about having a mother with facial hair.

I am telling you, I never wear it anywhere near my perianal or my vaginal-lips location. If it as much as touches my eyes, I wash them out with a solution. I promise you—*you are an angel*!—I keep it out of the reach of the children! **Q**

Ha

"See if you can find a whistle, even a toy whistle, *any* whistle," she implored.

He knew he'd never find one in their town. When you know how it will turn out, you feel tired. So do I.

There ought to be a brilliant portrayal of the homecoming—the boy with what? or with the lack of what? the matriarch to be reckoned with.

An hour later, the boy returned with nothing to say.

After her hesitation, his mother asked, "So?"

He heard her clanking their plates.

But instead of answering his mother, the boy went back out into the back yard.

Because the mother's confusion was even greater than her boy's, she said nothing more either. But oh, how she thought!

Oh, this is hopeless! she thought.

What would her boy's fate be? she wondered. Well, she decided, they need a victim. I need a victim. We all need a victim.

The boy's heart heaved. He thought he was confident of the future. His house had been through fire. Things needed doing.

As for his mother, her voice had positively no timbre. She barely got her words out. In real life, she was barely heard.

About other details—or more about the boy—I don't have any ambition for any more, except to observe that the boy squatted on his haunches in the flowers.

The mother remembered then—that, as a baby, he had looked a trace displeased to be born. **Q**

DIANE WILLIAMS

Naaa

There's the baby who gets the bee sting. In my opinion, there's the baby carrying around a paperweight that, if he had dropped it on his bare foot, would or could have broken his foot.

The mother of the babies has sprained her ankle, and chipped a bone in it, and she is using a cane to help her get around.

Here's where the plot is thickening. Here's the plot: When the baby was stung, at first no one was sure what had happened, but then the mother said, "His arm is getting all pink." Not to go on and on—the sting was discovered on the tip of the baby's thumb. Finally—I was there—at the moment of the discovery, when just then: the baby stopped his crying.

I was the person who took the paperweight away from the baby. He walks. He's old enough to walk, just old enough, which is why I call him a baby. He was disappointed, but did not appear outraged, when I took the paperweight away from him. "You should not be carrying this around," I said.

If this were an issue larger than the worry about human extinction, I could allow myself to think about it.

Secretly, I believe the paperweight is an item which should never have existed, *ever*.

The facts of the matter are complex, but this baby's power is nowhere limited.

This baby's power is his renunciation of all power. **Q**

DIANE WILLIAMS

The Fullness of Life Is from Something

Exploring the front of her blouse herself—she leaned her head down—her nose, her mouth, her eyes became unpleasantly close to the rest of her. She did not feel, however, disgust. Happily, she was imagining a dark rose-red rose on its black bed.

In her present mood, unfolding before her, she saw valleys and shadows upon herself with something else—we'll get back to that—introduced that she did not crave, that had nothing to do with the turmoil of her spirit, nor with her modest capacity as a person.

This was happening not purely by chance. What had happened was that she had said, "The roses are so beautiful."

"Do you want them?" he had said. "You paid for them."

Next thing, he was wrapping the three roses up for her to take with her. Next thing, she had thought about nipping a bud and wearing a bud. Next thing, she had thought about it again, more nipping—because she had not nipped any bud yet, nor had she put any bud behind her ear, nor fastened with a hairpin a bud into her hair, nor stuck a bud into a buttonhole on the front of her blouse, where a bud would barely make itself famous, because it was not a bud that would glow in the dark.

Next thing, when her sister was putting her face unpleasantly close to hers, she was uncomforted by the nearness of her sister, or by the apparent growing kindness of her sister, as her sister talked, talked, talked to her, as officially as her sister could manage to about the void. **Q**

DIANE WILLIAMS

The Time of Harmony, or Crudité

I would say I was half the way through when I thought to myself: Be careful. Anyway, there were twenty of them, to begin with.

I cut every one in half.

There were six.

I cut one to pieces, wedge-shaped. I'd say there were nine wedges. This is the estimate, generally, I get from thinking back on it.

I cut slices from it.

I'd say there were six slices.

I sawed and I sawed back and forth.

I cut stalks. I made chips. There were about fifty more wedges. There were wheels. One wheel which I had produced took off, rolled along, and dropped. I made sticks and I made slivers. I made raggedy bunches, stalks, chunks.

The house was neat and clean as ever. I got a lot of things done. I fully enjoyed sex. It turned out I was very deep into being.

On so many occasions, what goes with what? I do not want to leave behind anything during the accumulation that I will have to grasp at one glance because it is not a piece of crap. **Q**

DIANE WILLIAMS

The Band-Aid and the Piece of Gum

There was the possibility up until five o'clock—then there was no more possibility. I expected to hear from Walter today. When I woke up, I was cheered by the thought that maybe today, *today* would be the most important day of my life. Today I ended up using the Band-Aid Walter had given me on my toe. He had thrust it into my hand. "Take it. You never know when you may need it." The piece of gum he had once given me I chewed today finally also. "Try it. You could learn something" is what he had said. Remember how I told you he grabbed me around the neck the last time I saw him? It was practically impossible to walk, which he was trying to do all at the same time, and trying to get me to walk along with him, too. There was the possibility, perhaps, that we could both have toppled over onto his floor.

That's it. Usually they start where a person was born, then their parents, their parents' parents, where they were born, occupations, so that includes dates, names, locations, character traits of all the parties concerned, chronology, trauma, wishes, dreams, eccentricities, real speech, achievements, including struggle, the obstacles, someone's dementia, another chronic illness, a centrifugal drama, certainly all the deaths, photos, paintings if any—likenesses of many of the parties concerned, plus summary statements made periodically throughout to sum up the situation at any given time. **Q**

DIANE WILLIAMS

Torah

I carry this plate of triumph into the school building with my Saran Wrap all a-flutter all over my iced cakes. I have iced my cakes because I think everyone nowadays has an expectation of icing on it from a cupcake, as I am sure I do, too.

The corn candies I pushed into the icing are the tough lumps, my vicious triples, my quadruples, the repetition of an idea an idea an idea an idea an idea. Are you keeping track of this as I did? This situation could be handled.

I took control of the situation when the official in the office did nothing when she saw me create a situation in her office. But I gave up control when this official declared that no man had ever hooked his fingers into her vagina and then keenly observed her face, or pleaded to go down on her, or pushed her against a wall into her own shadow and said, "We call this dry humping when we do it in school!"

As it turned out, for no good reason, I tested the woman sorely.

I was wicked.

Yet perfectly delightful when I was God. **Q**

DIANE WILLIAMS

The Big Parade

The only beginning to this I can bear is "You weren't wearing any!" which a woman who would not hush herself in a restaurant declared. I am asserting she wanted to set another woman there straight, who, with some shame, I suppose, did not hesitate to put her hands up over her ears and to ask anyone at all, "Where are they?"

All of the above stirs me.

All of the above stirs me no more than does the most urgent matter in my own life. The damage is done.

With some difficulty, I could tell you more. I could name *you,* the unnamed you.

Here I am with what has happened. I am not now going to back up and go around to where this is supposed to end by rule, to where I would have to publicly proclaim my loss, as my husband did yesterday, hunched over, carrying my suitcases, headed with his head down—that attitude. I followed him down the big avenue, through the big parade—we cut right through it, and I followed, and there at the big hotel my husband said, "I want to take these inside for you!" and I followed him to where he delivered me personally, so passionately, to my next husband forthcoming.

I had a strangely tender attitude only toward myself then, not toward either one of them, which I have been told is the motive force behind anyone's pursuit of novelty. **Q**

DIANE WILLIAMS

The Leader

In just a little while I was not yet so weary that I was furiously working on the secret of life, of my life.

The words in my mouth are uncontrollable the way they come out to speak. Fluently I say: He is a Jew, but who am I?

The Jew laughed, and he said coercively, before he stripped himself naked, before he became the master of my body, before he tickled my slit, before he tugged on my slit, before he tugged it, before he tugged on it, before I was so hard on his hard-on—he said it coercively to me: "Don't be so silly."

"You must let go of me," I said.

Wisely, the Jew said, "This is what it always comes to."

I struggled to my feet. I was profusely kind, too, before going any further. Then the Jew got up, too. He is by temperament eager.

We were near a patch of trees where there was a family—I think a family excited by fury. Not one of them—the three little girls, a mother and a father—was in any way, shape, or form calm, or happy, or prepared quite yet to be the leader of the family.

Nor was that all: Underfoot, there were heavy tree roots popping up everywhere, and acorns, some crushed, some with, some without their tiny what-nots still on, all of which—this spectacle—was not useless to me, for I can speak for the Jew, too, such is my destiny, that in full daylight our eyes were open not with horror, not to see a fearful end, but to realize—I realize a certain sort of family should probably gather more often as a group to be a witness to love. It was thrilling when the youngest girl asked me, "Did you ever get caught before?"

"Well, sure," I answered her, "and up yours." **Q**

DIANE WILLIAMS

The Dog

She had every reason to think that he had had a good time with her when he licked thoroughly with his strong tongue the private parts of her body. She was in bed when he did this. He was her best friend.

When she awoke the next morning, she smelled the sweet lilac and the roses in her garden—she was aware of the thump of his tail—and felt a breeze spring in through the window screen.

She ate a small piece of fish for her breakfast. She hummed a little tune to herself—and when she opened a drawer, she observed an old crumb from some food in there and she thought, This is unbelievable.

Her husband, Frank, came in for his breakfast. Frank is clever, of course.

She said to Frank, *"Sit!"*

Really, she did not understand at that time why Frank didn't. **Q**

DIANE WILLIAMS

Machinery

He moves around in his gloom and then he does something with something. He is calmer about his longings.

He sits for a bit before he hears whatever it is. Hearing it gives him the sensation of holding on to a great instrument which is at work.

He discovers a small square white cardboard box and he opens it. Inside is a disappointment.

His children hold him responsible for everything he does. His house suits him.

For some idea of the full range of tools at his disposal, one would have to know what human longings are all about, a calm voice says calmly. **Q**

LYNN GROSSMAN

Raising Mom

Mackie tells Mom. Oh, what moaning. Oh, what crying, swooning to the floor, and so on and so on.

Women should not moan and cry on floor, says Mackie. A couch is better. Me, I would say floor. Nothing left to fall down onto from, but Mackie is older. You've got to go by Mackie.

We pick Mom up. Try to, that is, then quit. Mom is bigger on the floor swooned down moaning this way than she is standing up. Mackie and I just leave her there. I get the knitted thing off the couch and cover Mom.

This is Mackie: Get water! Get ice!

Mom looks her wet eyes up into Mackie's eyes and moans, Mackie, Mackie.

Water, Mom? Mackie says. Ice, Mom?

Now Mom's crying stops. Now no moaning, too, just the sounds of the TV on and the parakeets waiting for seed.

The skin around Mom's neck is going white to pink to white again, like a kind of wave. Mom's eyes leave Mackie's eyes and roll back into a place of their own, and what looks up at Mackie and me is white and nothing but white.

This is Mackie: Mom?

This is me: Mom?

Nothing is what we get back from Mom, just wet white roundness pointed in our direction.

Screaming, yelling, that's Mackie and me.

It's temporary, Mackie says.

Don't be so young, Mackie says.

Mackie tries to raise Mom. Mackie sprays Mom's jungle perfume from the tiger-skin bottle under Mom's nose. Mackie slaps Mom's face until the mark of Mackie's fingers shows on Mom's cheek.

We wait.

We wait.

Here's Mom: nothing, nothing, then more nothing.
Mackie says it: Mouth-to-mouth.
This is me: No way.
This is Mackie: Do it!
You! I say.
You! Mackie says, and we You! You! You! each other back and forth again.

Mackie stands up big, then bigger. Mackie gives me the famous Mackie look, a look that makes your knees want to bend, a look that lets you know that Mackie is the older one and you've got to go by Mackie.

Down on the floor I go, hands and knees over Mom. Oh, those round white eyes. Oh, that jungle smell. Oh, the curve of Mom's long neck coming from deep inside Mom's unbuttoned shirt.

I part Mom's mouth wide open. My mouth presses down on Mom's mouth, teeth click-clicking on Mom's teeth. Oh, the tastes—tasting smokes, tasting coffees, tasting teeth, tasting lipsticks, tasting Moms.

This is Mackie: Breathe!

Mom's tongue sleeps shy behind Mom's teeth. Move it aside with my tongue for easy air passing. My, the back of Mom's teeth are slippery smooth! Also front of Mom's teeth, also Mom's tongue, and so on and so on.

Breathe! Mackie says, Breathe! Mackie keeps telling me and Mackie keeps telling me, but Mackie is just wasting breath. With what I am doing, you cannot go by Mackie, you've got to go by Mom, by the way Mom's body moves, by the way Mom is breathing it back to you. Mackie gives me the famous Mackie look, but what do I care? I do not care.

I tell Mom. Everybody's got their own way of telling and I tell Mom hard. I breathe hard right into Mom. I talk the words right into Mom's throat, right down into inside Mom.

Mom's eyelids flutter. Oh, what a Mom-sized moan.

This is Mackie—but I do not listen. Why should I listen? I breathe out, Mom breathes in, Mom breathes out, I breathe in, back and forth this way—we're dancing breath to breath.

Is that Mackie's hand pushing my shoulder? Is that Mackie pulling my hair and my head and so on and so on? This is me: breathing and telling, breathing and telling Mom.

All of Mackie is on me now.

Wait your turn, Mackie.

Wait your fucking turn. **Q**

EILEEN HENNESSY

The Translator

I am a translator. I convert words written in French, German, Spanish, Dutch, and Italian into English. The way I do it makes it a mechanical act. Find an English equivalent for a foreign word. Write it down. Go on to the next word.

Some translators make things complicated. For example, take this translation from the German that I am doing for one of my clients, a lawyer who specializes in immigration cases. It is the birth certificate of Heinz M., German, born on 27 September 1942 in Kulm, District of Akkermann, Bessarabia. Mother: Bertha M., now residing in Hamburg, Federal Republic of Germany. Father: Theodor M., died on 3 September 1942 in Kulm.

Some people say a translator should take nothing for granted. He should do research, check spellings, names, dates, places, use the encyclopedia, the atlas, the dictionary. Such a translator would look up *Kulm* and *Akkermann* in the atlas to determine whether these German place-names should be appearing in Bessarabia. He would speculate on the possibility that Theodor M. was a German soldier who died at the Russian front, twenty-four days before the birth of the son in question. Such a translator would wonder why Theodor M.'s wife, a woman pregnant, was at the front.

This is not my method. Put down the word, go on to the next word: this is how I work.

I translate in my apartment.

My apartment is in a building that is owned by an eighty-two-year-old man named Saunders, whom I have never seen. The building, which is at least a hundred years old, is of the sort referred to in newspaper articles as "crumbling."

There are two apartments on every floor. Each apartment has its own kitchen, but they share a bathroom. My apartment is at the back of the building. When I look out, I see the windowless brick wall of a factory.

A new tenant recently moved into the front apartment on my floor. She is a tall, thin woman in her late seventies or early eighties, with a quantity of brownish-gray hair that she piles on top of her head. One of the other tenants told me that she is a retired college professor of English.

People are always moving in and out of this building, so I might never have noticed her but for the fact that she has a habit of leaving the bathroom door unlocked when she is sitting on the toilet. I have almost walked in on her three times.

Last week an attorney named Frank Schroeder gave me a French appellate court decision to translate. It is printed on two-column pages packed with fine print and is full of *Whereas* clauses that run on for paragraphs.

A French *Whereas* clause sounds like this: Considérant que le Ministère public demande à la Cour, par voie de conclusions écrites, de confirmer le jugement entrepris en ce qu'il affirme le caractère confidentiel d'une lettre échangée entre une banque et son client, quel que soit le cadre dans lequel elle l'a été, pourvu que son objet soit licite.

In other words, Whereas the Office of the Public Prosecutor has filed written pleadings with the Court praying for confirmation of the judgment rendered, insofar as it affirms the confidential nature of a letter exchanged between a bank and its customer regardless of the context in which it was so exchanged, provided that its purpose is lawful.

A Dutch *Whereas* clause sounds like this: Aangezien de kandidaat door een getuigschrift heeft bewezen: Whereas the candidate submitted a certificate showing that for at least two years, starting from the time he obtained the degree of Candidate in the Medical Sciences, he assiduously and successfully worked in the medical, surgical, and obstetrical clinics.

An Italian *Whereas* clause sounds like this: Premesso che l'Assemblea dei Soci ha deliberato: Whereas the General Meeting of Shareholders deliberated on an action of liability against the director, and whereas, consequently, he was dismissed from office pursuant to Section Three of Article Two thousand three hundred ninety-three of the Civil Code.

A Spanish *Whereas* clause sounds like this: Considerando que mediante Acuerdo Gubernativo: Whereas by Government Ruling Number Three hundred fifty-nine dash twenty-four of May eighth, as amended by Government Ruling Number Nine hundred seventy-two dash thirty-four of June second and Government Ruling Number Two thousand four hundred ninety-five dash sixteen of July fourth, the model for the contract of participation in oil production was approved.

Whereas clauses can be very complicated and full of dependent clauses and vague words. Very often, we translators tidy them up so that the client reading our translation never realizes just how nearly incomprehensible the original clause was.

Frank Schroeder has large arms that look made for fighting or farming, not for holding law books. We have gone out together several times.

       We translators render.

I learned this word early in my childhood. There was a company in our town that collected scraps of fat from the butcher shops and took them to a factory where they were rendered for grease.

CERTIFICATION OF ACCURACY

This is to certify that I———have *rendered* the document appended hereto from the———language into the———language; and that my translation is, to the best of my knowledge and ability, a true and correct *rendering* of the original document written in———.

I see my new neighbor downstairs in the vestibule as I am on my way out to the bank one morning. She is wearing a blue polyester suit, black patent-leather shoes with very high heels, and a broad-brimmed white hat with a bunch of cloth violets pinned to the crown, and she is lighting a fresh cigarette from the end of a cigarette she is holding.

We do not speak to each other. She goes up the street in one direction, I go in the other.

My street is an east-west street lined with four- and five-story brick-and-brownstone apartment houses built about a hundred years ago. Each building has a metal fire escape that starts at the roof and descends past the front windows to the second story, where there is a ladder that can be lowered to the ground. The fire-escape windows are barricaded with gates, the ground-floor windows are barred with rods. Metal garbage cans stand along the curb. The side wall of one building is covered with a mural of neighborhood scenes.

Several north-south avenues cross my street. The avenue to the west of my apartment has a candy store, three bars, an Off-Track Betting office, a delicatessen, a parking lot, and a small park with benches, children's swings and slides, and four basketball courts. Groups of young men stand around on the corners, sit in the park, or walk up and down the sidewalks.

The avenue to the east has a delicatessen, a supermarket, a laundromat, two drugstores, a butcher store, several fruit and vegetable stores. All the stores have sliding metal gates across their fronts. During the day, most of the storekeepers slide the gates back just far enough to let customers enter. The only exception is Tom, the manager of the laundromat, who leaves his gates wide open all day long.

The laundromat has twenty machines, a public telephone, and four metal folding chairs. The windows, the walls, and the black plastic floor are always damp. The moisture trickles down the windows.

The laundromat is busy sixteen hours a day, seven days a week. I usually go there around seven o'clock on a weekday morning, before it gets crowded. First I buy a container of coffee in the delicatessen. Then I sit on one of the metal folding chairs and drink the coffee and watch my clothes go around in the machine.

My bank is also in the avenue to the east of my apartment. It is a modern international bank with machines that accept deposits, dispense money, and accept payment of bills. There are computer terminals connected with the bank's central computer, and tellers to wait on people who do not wish to use the machines, with a blinking light to direct customers to the tellers who are free to wait on them.

Every time I go to the bank, I think about computers. I also think about computers every time I get together with my friend Pauline, who is a computer systems analyst for this bank and an enthusiast of everything connected with computers.

Pauline has a one-bedroom apartment in a new building that has an elevator. She always tells me I should find a new apartment.

"The place where you live is a slum," she says. "You need a nice place you can call home."

My oil-company client has given me a drilling contract to be translated from Spanish.

The contract begins with an explanation.

Después del análisis correspondiente y contando con el informe acerca de la capacidad técnico-financiera del oferente, y con base en lo dispuesto en el numeral uno del Artículo Nueve del Acuerdo de Convocatoria, el Comité de Calificación acepta la oferta presentada por la compañía, y como consecuencia adjudica los bloques que integran el area del contrato objeto de la convocatoria y que comprende una superficie total de ciento cinco mil doscientas tres hectáreas con treinta y ocho centésimas de hectárea.

In other words, Having performed the appropriate analysis and studied the report on the bidder's technical and financial capabilities, based on the provisions of Section One of

Article Nine of the Call for Bids, the Bid Award Committee accepts the offer submitted by the Company, and consequently awards it the blocks that constitute the contract area concerned in the call for bids, consisting of a total of one hundred five thousand two hundred three and thirty-eight one-hundredths hectares.

The parties then state that they have decided to enter into a Contrato de Operaciones Petroleras de Explotación, a Petroleum Exploitation Operations Contract, that is to be signed between the Minister of Energy and the company.

The parties state their names and give some information about themselves. This is not as short and simple as it sounds. In this contract, the first party is Alejandro A., age forty, married, domiciled in this city, representing the Government of the Republic, acting in his capacity as Minister of Energy, which said capacity he evidences with the appointment contained in Government Decision Number one hundred seven of September tenth, One thousand nine hundred eighty-three and Instrument Number Thirty dash eighty-three, indicating that he assumed said post.

The second party is Carlos H., age fifty-nine, married, accountant, domiciled in this city, acting in his capacity as General Agent with Power of Representation for the Y Company, a company established under the Laws of the Republic, which said capacity he evidences with a certified photocopy of Official Instrument Number One hundred forty, certified in this city on October seventh, one thousand nine hundred seventy-six by a Notarial Attorney, and duly recorded in the General Register of Instruments under Number Thirteen thousand three hundred seventy-seven, and in the General Trade Register of the Republic under Number Eight thousand nine hundred twenty-three, page seventy-two of Book Ten of Trade Registers.

These are fairly short descriptions of the parties. I have translated descriptions that went on for pages, through lengthy citations of every official register in which any information concerning the party had ever been recorded.

The description of a drilling area begins like this:

Bloque Q guión cinco guión setenta y dos, el cual se describe así: Partiendo del punto de intersección del meridiano noventa grados con cincuenta y uno minutos y veinte y ocho segundos, con el paralel diez y siete grados con treinta y seis minutos y treinta y ocho segundos, se sigue el paralel rumbo este, hasta su intersección con el meridiano noventa grados con cuarenta y uno minutos y veinte segundos.

That is, Block Q dash five dash seventy-two, described as follows: Starting from the point of intersection of meridian ninety degrees fifty-one minutes thirty-eight seconds, following the parallel due eastward to its intersection with meridian ninety degrees forty-one minutes and twenty seconds.

And so on for a page or more. There must be no room for doubt that the parties are who they are claiming to be, and that the site being drilled is the one described in the contract.

Once, I had four oil-company clients, all of them entering into book-length contracts with various governments.

Pauline telephones me when I about halfway through the drilling contract.

"There's an apartment listed in the Apartments for Rent section of the newspaper," she says. "It sounds good. Why not take a break from translating and go look at it?"

She reads the ad to me. Studio with terrace, fireplace, loft bed, quiet elevator building, charming tree-lined street, convenient location. Superintendent on the premises.

I decide to look at it.

My neighbor is in the vestibule, smoking.

"Hello, I'm your neighbor," I say. "I live in the rear apartment."

My neighbor turns her head, takes the cigarette out of her mouth, says, "Yes, I know you," she says. "No, that's the wrong word. I *recognize* you. That's the right word. Accuracy in language is important."

She takes a pack of cigarettes out of her bag and lights a fresh cigarette from the cigarette she is holding.

"I come down here to smoke because the air in my apartment is so bad," she explains.

"Isn't it dangerous to smoke so much?" I ask.

"Oh, we all have things we do to make the time pass," she says. "Some people go to their offices, some people smoke, some people drink. Activities that make our lives pass, you know what I mean. That's all we can do about life, after all, make it pass. You, now," she suddenly points a finger at me, "what do you do to make your life pass?"

"I translate," I say.

"What?"

"I take texts written in foreign languages and turn them into English."

"Oh, I see," she says. "Well, I suppose that's as good an activity as anything else. But what do you actually *do* when you translate?"

"Well, it involves working with words," I say.

"Yes, yes, I already know that," she says. "Texts are made of words. Foreign words, English words, it's all the same. It sounds to me as if multiplication is what you do. You take one text and make it into two. Multiplication, I call that."

"Well, I guess that's one way . . ."

"But that doesn't explain what you do," she interrupts. "Always explain yourself clearly. Accuracy in language is important. It's the only way to avoid misunderstandings."

Abruptly she opens the street door and goes out without another look at me. She goes up the street in one direction, I go in the other.

The four-story apartment building is plain, clean but not sparkling, and in need of painting inside and out. The halls are lighted by fluorescent tubes. The elevator is out of order.

The apartment is at the rear of the building. It has a

terrace and a sleeping loft, and it is quiet, small, and rather dark. The windows of the neighboring apartment look onto the terrace. There is a wood-burning stove in a corner.

I tell the superintendent I shall telephone him as soon as I have made a decision.

Pauline calls me later. "Well, how was it?"

"All right," I say.

"What does that mean?"

"Nothing," I say. "It was nothing special, that's all."

"Why don't you come over to my house for dinner tonight," she says. "We can look at the apartment rental ads and make a plan for you to follow. Also, I have a French magazine article that I want you to translate for me."

I go back to the oil-company contract. I have reached the point at which the parties are agreeing on the length of time during which the contract will be in effect, and what will happen when it comes to an end.

Vigencia y plazo del contrato. El plazo del presente contrato es de veinticinco años, computados a partir de la fecha de vigencia a menos que termine por el acaecimiento de las causales establecidas en la ley o las estipulaciones de este contrato.

Inception and term of the Contract. The term of this Contract shall be twenty-five years, computed from the date of inception, unless it is terminated by virtue of the occurrence of one of the causes specified in the law or in the stipulations of this Contract. At the end of the evaluation phase, provided the Contractor has performed the obligations relative thereto, the Contractor shall have the option of giving up one or more of the exploitation blocks or the entire Contract area. The Contractor may select and retain for each commercial field an area not to exceed ten thousand hectares. When for any reason commercial production ends in any exploitation area, the Contractor must return the area in question.

. . .

At Pauline's house, after dinner, I see that her French magazine article is about the home of the future and how it will have computer-controlled automation on every floor. Until now there has been no overall control and information system for the home. The builders of apartment houses and individual homes are still operating as in the past, without taking into account the arrival of new technologies. But the manufacturers have plans for what will be the home of the future.

The various projects make the home the center of a computer-controlled system that regulates all the home appliances—the telephone, the microcomputer, the telecopier, and the television set; as well as the machines involved in the maintenance and comfort of the house—the air-conditioning units and the heating, washing, and cooking equipment. The "automated house" includes all the activities that are made possible by home computer terminals: making purchases from home, working at home, home-study courses with access to data banks of texts, sounds, and pictures, and the obtaining of all kinds of information: public transportation schedules, entertainment listings, and bank account statements.

"Just think of being able to go to the stores and the bank without leaving the house," Pauline says. "Meanwhile, *you* don't even have a nice place to live in."

We sit down with the newspaper advertisements and work out a plan for my search. Pauline tells me the things I should look for and the things I should be careful of and the things I should and should not say.

"Remember," she says as I am leaving, "you won't find something unless you look, and looking for an apartment in this city isn't easy. It's a landlord's market here."

Whenever I hear the word *market*, I think about my visit to Chichicastenango, a market town in the mountains of Guatemala. On market day, stalls are set up in the main square, in front of the church that stands at the top of a long flight of stairs. Hundreds of Indians come in from the nearby mountain villages to buy and sell goods.

Two days after my visit to the town, I read in a newspaper that an earthquake had killed and injured thousands of Indians and left thousands of others homeless. The hotel where I had stayed, the newspaper reported, was split in half.

That is what I think of whenever I hear the word *market*.

Whenever I hear the word *superintendent*, I think of Ludwik, the superintendent of my building, and his wife, Teresa, who came to this country from Poland a year ago. Ludwik is a thin man with curly brown hair that stands up all over his head. His wife is taller and bigger than he is, and she wears thick glasses. She does all the cleaning and much of the minor repair work in the building, and she also acts as Ludwik's interpreter when he has to speak with a tenant. Teresa speaks German better than English, so when she wants to tell me something, she often says it in German if she does not know the English words.

That is what I think when I hear *superintendent*.

Whenever I see Ludwik, I think about the afternoon when I saw him standing in front of one of the fruit and vegetable stores in the avenue, sketching the fruits and vegetables and flowers with pastel crayons.

"Very beautiful colors," he said, waving his hand at the bins on the sidewalk. "So many orange, yellow, green, red. Pink and blue flowers, how you call them? Tulips. Color, color, everything color."

My neighbor invites me into her apartment one day.

Her apartment gets more light than mine because it faces the street. It has the same layout: a room with two windows in the front wall, a small kitchen fitted into a recess in the rear wall opposite the windows. She has furnished it with a folding table, a folding chair, and a mattress on the floor.

Every time I meet her she talks about words. Yesterday she asked me again what I do when I translate.

"I have the feeling you don't realize what you're doing with those words," she said.

    Frank Schroeder wants a translation of an article about hotel concierges, "les hommes aux clés d'or," the men with golden keys. "What the customer wants, the customer gets" is their motto.

In a police raid on a hotel, one of the night concierges is arrested. The police find on him a little notebook containing the names of some thirty young women. The Vice Squad claims that he is at the center of a network that allegedly includes the most prestigious Paris hotels.

Frank Schroeder is particularly interested in the story of L., one of the girls listed in the night concierge's notebook. She had been working the leading Paris hotels for ten years. Now she sits and waits beside the telephone in her studio condominium.

"I started in the hotels ten years ago," L. tells the writer of the article. "I was just filling in for my girl friend C., who had given my number to the hotel concierge. I've been at it ever since."

"How much do you give the concierge?" the writer asks.

"My girl friend kicked back three or four hundred francs a trick, depending on what kind of client it was. Now it's up to six hundred."

"What does the concierge do to earn a kickback that large?" the writer asks.

"Well, lots of times it's the concierge who negotiates the price of the trick with the client," L. says. "It's okay with me, he deserves it. So do I. It's true that I make a good living. But I earn every penny of it, believe me. At least I did." She looks at the telephone, which has not rung.

"How much?" the writer asks.

"Twelve to fourteen million francs a month. But my business expenses run me between five and six million. What with this studio, the hairdresser, and a manicure every other day, cosmetic surgery, tips, sales taxes . . . And then there's the fines! Last year the tax guys dropped the net on me during an investigation. When those boys catch you, you pay, brother!"

"Still, it's better than being a cleaning woman, isn't it?" the writer asks.

"Look, mister, don't fucking kid around, okay?" L. says.

"Nice apartment you have here," the writer says.

"It cost me a bundle, let me tell you. But it's better than renting. The landlords practically double the rent when they know the apartment is for girls like us. One girl friend of mine—all the tenants in the building ganged up on her. Did all kinds of things, throwing cans of paint on her car, putting cement in her lock, ruining her coat. They filmed her clients with a little videocamera. 'We're going to send the cassette to your wife,' they'd yell at the john."

L. worries about how she will earn her living from now on. "I may not be able to keep this apartment," she tells the writer. "And what with the housing shortage in this city . . ."

I start with the first apartment on the list that Pauline and I worked out. The advertisement says it is a beautiful studio with alcove, in up-and-coming neighborhood, with brand-new kitchen and bathroom fixtures, exposed brick wall, fireplace, won't last long at this rent in this neighborhood.

The neighborhood consists of different types of buildings, most of them in about the same condition as my building, some of them abandoned and boarded up, some of them in the process of being renovated and improved.

The apartment for rent is on the fifth floor of one of the renovated buildings. There is no elevator. The kitchen and bathroom fixtures are new. The owner has created the alcove by building a closet that projects out into the room from one of the side walls. The other side wall is exposed brick, with a small fireplace.

"We make no representations as to the usability of the fireplace," the managing agent tells me. "You will have to determine this yourself. We believe, however, that it was designed merely to take the pipe of a coal stove."

I thank him for showing me the apartment.

One of my clients brings me a lease and a building manager's contract for translation from French.

The contract describes the duties that the manager must perform: Coordination of all maintenance services, relations with the owners and the occupants of the building, maintenance of general accounting records, inspection and supervision of premises and of proper maintenance of the equipment, day-to-day maintenance and repair of installations, assignment and supervision of personnel in charge of building security and fire safety.

"Never mind that," my client says. "What I want to know is the rent. Tell me what the lease says about my rent."

Subject to change pursuant to the index of retail prices published by the Minister of Economic Affairs, the rent is set at one hundred thousand francs per année, which the lessee promises to pay in advance in quarterly installments covering the first, second, third, and fourth calendar quarters, respectively. A first payment covering the period up to the first quarter shall be made upon signing of this lease. Any and all taxes, levies, and contributions in general assessed or to be assessed by any authority whatsoever relative to the leased premises or to their occupancy or assigned use shall be payé exclusively by the lessee.

"The bloody frogs," my client says.

After he leaves, I sit at my typewriter for a while, looking out at the factory wall.

I get off at the bus stop near the corner of my street. I have been shopping. I have bought too many things, and with all my bags and bundles I have to fight my way through the crowded bus to get off. My handbag is dangling by its strap.

Halfway up my street, I stop to shift bags. Suddenly I feel a hard tug on my handbag. Then I see a small, thin man running up the street ahead of me, running very fast. My handbag, its strap looped around the handle of one of my shopping bags, is still dangling.

"That neighborhood is getting too dangerous," Pauline says. "Look, do me a favor. Today. Now. Get the Apartments for Rent section of the paper and pick out a few ads. Then take a few hours off and go look at them. Please?"

The most exciting rental opportunity you've ever had. Super studio. Separate kitchen, wood-burning fireplace, hardwood floors. Immediate occupancy.

Lovely, livable one-bedroom in elevator building, carpeted halls, new kitchen, twenty-four-hour protection.

Elegant sunny one-bedroom, gallery entrance, separate raised dining area, high ceilings.

A separate kitchen is created by placing cabinets or standalone closets opposite the wall where the kitchen fixtures are installed so as to separate them from the rest of the room. A wood-burning fireplace is a metal stove installed in one corner of the room. A raised dining area is a platform raised about two inches off the floor. In a twenty-four-hour-protection system, a television camera is mounted near the street door.

On my way home, I meet my next-door neighbor.

"I'm going to have a glass of beer in one of the bars," she says. "Won't you join me?"

"I have a lot of work to do," I say.

"It won't hurt you to take an hour off," my neighbor says. "The bar I go to is an old-time neighborhood place. There aren't many of them left nowadays. Why not come along and take a look? We won't stay long."

The bar is a brick building in the avenue west of my house, the avenue with the candy store, three bars, betting office, delicatessen, parking lot, and park. From the window I can see the park with the swings and slides and basketball courts and the young men sitting and lying on the benches.

My neighbor and I find a space at one side of the bar and order two steins of beer.

"Is it always this crowded on weekday afternoons?" I ask.

"Usually," my neighbor says. "You should see it here on Friday nights—you can hardly get in, it's so packed with people. On Saturday afternoons, a little band sets up at the back and plays all the old-time dance tunes, and everybody gets out on the floor and dances. It reminds me of my younger days, when there was a place like this on practically every corner."

"There aren't many young people here," I say.

"I don't know where the young people go today," my neighbor says. "They certainly don't come to places like this. I know every old-fashioned bar up and down this avenue, and I don't see young people in any of them. Refill, please," she calls out to the bartender, gesturing at her empty stein.

She begins to describe the neighborhood bars of her youth. Very respectable places they were, she says, with singing and dancing on Fridays and Saturdays. The bartenders were the lords of the manor, she says, and the police, who were called Cossacks in those days, hauled away the men who became intoxicated. I listen to her and drink my beer and watch the people resting their feet on the brass footrail or standing around in groups or sitting at the tables along the walls.

My neighbor is still telling her story when we both become aware of a commotion in one corner of the room. Several people have gathered around a man who is lying on the floor.

"Probably drank too much," my neighbor says. "It happened in the past, it happens today, it will go on happening in the future. As long as a man doesn't get so obstreperous that the bartender has to call the police, there's no harm done."

One of the people standing over the man who is lying on the floor goes to a telephone and makes a call.

"What will happen to this man?" I ask.

"Oh, some of his friends will help him get home," my neighbor says. "It's not a problem. Even people who are totally out of control seem to hang on to their sense of how to get home. I remember my brother telling me about the time he drank too many martinis and was totally and completely gone and out, and still he was able to get on the train and find his way home."

She describes the martinis and the people her brother was with that night and how they all drank too much but her brother was the only one who was so affected. I listen to her and drink my beer and look at the man on the floor.

"He never touched another martini after that night," my neighbor says. "So you see the impression the experience made on him. Because he was terribly sick for two days afterward, that's why. Beer is all right, no harm done with beer. Champagne can give you a terrible headache. Champagne on top of wine is as bad as martinis. Another bad thing is to mix the fruit of the vine with the fruit of the grain. Never mix, dear. Mixing is what kills you. Listen to me."

An ambulance pulls up in front of the bar. Its rotating lights move around the walls of the room. Two men jump out, grab a stretcher, and come into the bar. An Oriental man carrying a black bag gets out and follows them.

"The hospitals around here employ a lot of Oriental doctors," my neighbor says.

The Oriental man kneels down, takes a stethoscope out of his bag, and listens first at the fallen man's chest, then at various other points on the man's body. After a few minutes, the Oriental man raises his head and looks around the room. Then he stands up and says something to the ambulance attendants, who place the fallen man on the stretcher and put a sheet over his body and over his face. They move through the crowd toward the door, with the Oriental man following them. No one goes with them to the ambulance.

"A soul has passed," my neighbor says.

"It happened so quietly," I say.

"I remember the time I was caught in an earthquake," my neighbor says. "What amazed me was that the sun went on shining and the sky was still blue and the birds kept right on chirping while it was happening. Everything was completely normal."

We have another stein of beer, and then we leave.

Translation of a travel brochure about Europe:

In Europe, neighborhood bars are known as cafés. They are meeting places where people go to relax and talk. The first cafés were already operating in Arabia by the fifteenth century. From there they spread to Constantinople, in 1555, and to Venice around 1640. The first café in France was opened in Marseille in 1654. The first café in Paris was opened by Gregory of Aleppo and by a Sicilian named Procopio, and was frequented by Voltaire.

Around 1770, the first cafés-concerts were opened in Paris. The café-concert was a music hall where the public could drink, smoke, and listen to comic songs and skits. Paris also had café-théâtres, cafés for the performance of improvisational works and plays that for one reason or another did not fit into the format of traditional theater.

The cafés were frequented by writers, and specifically by a new type of writer who lived by his pen instead of being supported by royalty. In the literary worlds of Madrid and Paris and other leading European cities, every writer had his favorite café, and the influence of café life can be seen dans les works of numerous writers. Every European country has its own equivalent of the café, the coffeehouse, the neighborhood bar where people meet to talk and drink and relax for a while.

There is a European computer so efficace that it can store up to forty-one million two hundred thousand characters. In other words, up to twenty thousand typed pages of data and text can be stored in its memory. A simple little key allows the user to lock the computer securely, so that the information in its memory is protected.

European cars are said to be characterized by revolutionary mechanics, resolutely original design, and daring aesthetics. They are cars that are exceptional from every point of view, objects that are as nice to look at as they are to experience and drive. These cars represent, in an understatedly elegant manner, supreme dynamism based on exclusive technology and technical systems. They are cars that reveal the demanding nature and individualism of the persons who drive them, because to buy a first-class car requires a certain financial independence.

Expensive European cars do not come through my street, which does not have much automobile traffic, in any case. My street is a street that people walk through in order to reach one of the avenues.

"Every computer is a real system," Pauline says to me as we are eating dinner. "Even a simple one. The computer is where it all starts. Have you looked at any more apartments?"

"Not this week," I say.

"You're not going to find anything if you don't look," Pauline says.

"I had so much work this week that I didn't have time."

Outside the restaurant, a man in a tattered coat and with hair down to his shoulders approaches us and asks for money. Pauline puts a dollar bill into his cup.

"A former translator," she says to me. "At one time he was the best translator of Spanish in the city."

Pauline makes this kind of joke every time we pass one of the homeless people in the street.

From this point following the meridian due north to its intersection with parallel seventeen degrees twenty-five minutes exactly; from this point following the parallel due west to its intersection with meridian ninety degrees forty-seven minutes twenty segundos; from this point following the meridian due north to its intersection con parallel seventeen degrees twenty-eight minutes thirty-four seconds; from this point following due south I see the windowless brick rear wall of a factory in the next street.

    Dutch death certificate of S.R., a widow who died a few months ago in Holland. De overledene is een dochter van M.R. en B.D. De aangifte is gedaan door L.B., uitvaartleider, oud zevenenveertig jaar, die verklaarde uit eigen wetenschap kennis te dragen van het overlijden.
    The decedent is a daughter of M.R. and B.D. The declaration of death was filed by L.B., age forty-seven, funeral director, who declared that he knew of the death through his own personal knowledge.
    This is not what the Dutch words actually say.
    The Dutch words really translate as:
    The overled is a daughter of M.R. and B.D. The giving to was done by L.B., old forty-seven-year, outward-navigation leader, who declared out of own knowing knowledge to carry of the overleading.
    The Dutch refer to the deceased as overleds, people who have been led over, and to funeral directors as outward-navigation leaders, people who lead them over.
    There is a modern philosophical or literary movement that tears language apart like this to get at how people really think. A computer is useful for this purpose.

    I am on my way to the laundromat. It is shortly before seven o'clock in the morning, a time when few people are out in my street. Ahead of me, I see a young man in dungarees and a sweatshirt cross to the other side of the street and speak to a man. Then I realize that one of the men is holding a knife. I can hear the men arguing. I keep on walking.

. . .

"That's the last straw," Pauline says. "Now we absolutely have to move you out of there. Get ready for an all-out apartment-hunting campaign. In fact, from now on, I'm going to ask you for a weekly report on what you've looked at."

Memo by the oil company to the Ministry recapitulando the interexchange of documents concerning the question of the Ministry's granting of a credit a favor de the contractor relative to the obligatory expenses for the construction and maintenance of highways.

"I don't know what *interexchange* means," my client says. "Maybe you meant to say *exchange*? Also, I believe you made two typing errors. *Recapitulando* should be *recapitulating*, and I think *a favor de* should read *in favor of*."

The local chapter of our national translators' association is sponsoring one-day seminars on various topics of interest to translators. One of them is "The Translator and the Computer."

"Don't miss it," Pauline says, when I tell her about it. "You should think about getting a computer. It would make your work a lot easier."

A typewriter is good enough for a translator, with daisy wheels that can be changed quickly, because they come in super-practical drop-in cassettes. The electronic conveniences include a forty-stroke correction storage memory, which guarantees error-free typing. Forty-six character keys, a repeat key for all character and function keys, tab-set and tab-clear keys, a lift-off system, and more: in short, a typing marvel. Computers and typewriters, lawyers and translators, all work with words. Accuracy in language is important.

The auditorium is crowded for the lecture on "The Translator and the Computer." The first speaker explains, in simple terms, the operations a computer can perform. She is followed by a man who demonstrates the use of the computer as a dictionary for storing vocabulary in several languages.

Then a man demonstrates how a computer translates. He sits down at the keyboard and feeds a Spanish text into the computer, which has been programmed with vocabulary and grammar in Spanish and English. We wait while the computer prints out a translation, which the woman reads aloud.

The computer made a lot of mistakes, particularly with idiomatic expressions, phrases that could be interpreted in several ways, and words and sentence structures that had not been programmed into it beforehand. We all agree that its translation is too poor to be given to a client without editing.

The woman explains that translations done by a computer always have to be edited by a human translator. Someone in the audience remarks that this must slow down the flow of work, and challenges the computer to a race. A text is found, and the challenger and the computer go to work on it. The challenger wins, producing a finished translation long before the computer finishes printing out. There is a discussion about the advantages of the two methods.

As we are leaving the building, a man in torn jacket and trousers comes up to me and asks for money. "A former translator," someone in the group says. "Used to specialize in French and German."

When I go into the bathroom the next morning, I find a set of metal shelves standing in the bathtub.

"My newest treasure," my neighbor explains when I ask her about it. "Marvelous piece of furniture, isn't it? I found it outside a store. I've put it in the bathroom until I can decide where it looks best. What do you think?"

We make space for it against one of her walls. I help my neighbor maneuver it out of the bathtub and around the piles of papers and objects on her floor. "Perfect place for it," she says after we have moved it into position. "Now I'll have to get some things to put on the shelves."

I tell her about the seminar.

"Computers can't think," my neighbor says. "That's one of their major problems. Always be accurate in your thinking, dear. Accuracy in thinking is important."

"You program the computer with the vocabulary and grammar and syntax of the two languages," I explain to Pauline. "Next, you type the foreign-language text into the computer. Then you push a key to start the translating process. In a few minutes, the printer starts printing out the translation."

Pauline begins to talk about electrical and neuronal impulses, cognitive science, deductive reasoning versus intuitive recognition of analogies, hard-wired versus programmed. In no time I lose track of what she is saying.

"I don't understand any of this," I say.

"Think apartments," Pauline says. "What are you going to look at this week?"

Lovely sun-drenched one-bedroom. Tree-lined street. Central air conditioning. Available immediately.

The apartment is in the rear on the fourth floor of a walk-up building. The sunlight comes in over a parking lot between two tall buildings in the next street. The kitchen and bathroom fixtures are not new, but they are clean.

"We require three months' rent as a security deposit," the renting agent says.

"I see," I say.

"What do you do for a living?" the agent asks.

"I'm a translator."

"What?"

"I'm a translator."

"What's that?" the agent asks.

"I translate documents written in foreign languages into English."

"Oh," says the agent. "What company do you work for?"

"I don't work for any company," I say. "I'm self-employed."

"Oh," says the agent. "In that case, we require four months' security deposit. And we'll need to see copies of your tax returns for the past three years."

"I'll give you a tip," Pauline says. "When you see a parking lot between buildings, you can be pretty sure that it's just temporary and that pretty soon an office building will go up on the site."

"Watch the typos," Frank Schroeder says. "Lately I'm catching a lot of them in your translations. I can't submit sloppy work in court, you know."

The checkout line in the supermarket in the avenue to the east of my house is moving slowly. It is Saturday morning, and the store is very crowded. The checkout clerk is a woman I have never seen before. The man in front of me keeps shifting from one foot to another and inching his shopping cart forward. The cart bumps the back of the woman standing in front of him. She turns around and asks him to keep his cart where it belongs. He tells her to move up to where she belongs instead of hanging back and making the line longer than it already is. The woman says an obscenity. The man answers with another obscenity. The checkout clerk tells the two of them to be quiet if they do not want her to call the manager. The man tells the clerk to go ahead and call the manager, because he wants to make a complaint about the slowness of the service. The clerk tells the man that if he does not like the service in this store he can go somewhere else. The man leaves his cart, walks up to the cash register, and tries to punch the clerk, who screams. The manager appears and asks what is the problem. The man is screaming obscenities about the clerk and the line and the service. The manager asks the man to leave the store. The man kicks a display case standing near the cash register. The case collapses, scattering the merchandise all over the aisle. From where I am standing, I can see the owner of the fruit and vegetable store on the other side of the street opening the metal gate of his store.

    Weekly report.
One-bedroom apartment in beautiful, newly renovated building on one of the loveliest blocks in up-and-coming neighborhood. Loft bed, exposed brick wall, new kitchen and bathroom fixtures.

The apartment is on the second floor, in the rear. The bathroom is right near the door. The living room and the bedroom are connected by a small passage that contains the kitchen appliances. The ceilings are low. The windows have gates across them because they open onto the fire escape. The surrounding buildings are taller and shut out the light, so that the apartment is dark.

    Gesamteindruck der Einrichtung. Overall impression of our Einrichtung. Please check off the comments that apply. Then mail this postage-frei carte to our main apartment in Hamburg.

Sehr gut, repräsentative, mit allem sehr zufrieden. Very good, impressive, I was satisfied with everything. Gut, angenehm, recht nett, positive. Gut, pleasant, just fine, I have a positive impression. Akzeptable, gerade recht, nichts auszusetzen, in Ordnung, ganz normal. Acceptable, no criticism, everything in proper order. Leicht enttäuschend, muss nicht, könnte aber besser sein, etwas schlicht, wenig imposant, etwas klein geraten. Somewhat disappointing, könnte be better although improvement not absolutely necessary, a little on the plain side, not very imposing, mediocre. Enttäuschend, mickrig, provinzielle, provisorisch, entspricht nicht Image. Disappointing, skimpy, small-town, improvised, does not accord with the company's image.

EILEEN HENNESSY

. . .

Translation of a magazine article by an Italian economist on technological modernization and its socio-economic consequences.

Questa nostra epoca pena sarà ricordato como l'epoca della rivoluzione tecnologica. La tecnologia è al centro di attenzioni, entusiasmi, timori. Articoli, studi, dibattiti si stanno diffondendo in tutti i nostri paesi ad una velocità ancora maggiore di quanto non si diffonda la tecnologia stessa.

Our age will be remembered as the age of the technological revolution. Technology is the center of public attenzione, enthusiasm, and fear. Articles, studies, and discussions are spreading through the Western fears at a pace even faster than the speed with which technology itself is aging.

As regards the possibility offered by technology for a thorough remodeling of our organizational culture, we are still only at the beginning of our discoveries. We are on the way to becoming computer-assisted entusiasmi, countries capable of utilizing the imminent second technological revolution, networks with a thin country that is rudimentary but is nevertheless organized with modern attentionized systems of programming, management, and control.

One system fits into another, and that one fits into another, and another fits into another. We are experiencing a transition from "monadic" structures to systemic networks and a systemic vision. There has been a shift to integrating management-information systems and data processing. The integration of information systems, the integration of the various flows of revolution existing in our era, are important goals, and information is now recognized as a strategic asset. Systemic integration of fears for apartments now is. A plan is right from the furniture, which including the Sectional System living-room set and the Sectional System kitchen and the System two-bedroom set. This is systemic automatic and control of the home.

. . .

"Everyone has computerized systems now," Pauline says.

"Systems for what?" I say.

"For managing and controlling things," she says. "For distribution of goods, management of offices, planning of highways. Just about everything can be systemized. It's called systemic integration, or production integration, or the systemic approach, depending on what's involved."

"I see," I say.

"The next step is to design a computer that can think like a human being," Pauline says. "I hope you've been looking at apartments."

Weekly report.

Beautiful one-bedroom, ideally located near park, gourmet shops, fine restaurants, all transportation. Immediate occupancy. No fee.

Studio. Separate kitchen. Exclusive. Luxury doorman building. Prime lease.

Small studio, kitchen fixtures positioned to create an alcove near the door, with small window too high to look out of. Two small windows in the room. At the front of the building. Fire escapes on all windows.

"I think we'll have to get Teresa up here to fix that leak in the bathroom sink," my neighbor says.

"Yes, it's getting worse," I say. "You're right, we'd better do something about it."

"If you're busy with work, I'll go down and talk to her," my neighbor says.

"No, I'll go," I say. "Just in case she maybe wants to speak German."

Teresa herself answers when I knock on her door. I explain about the leak.

"Okay, I come up," she says. "Moment. Please come in."

She disappears into the kitchen. From where I stand in the living room, I can see a small room with a bed and a chest of drawers. Canvases, both white and painted, lean against the walls of the living room. Stained rags, palettes, and pots of paint are scattered about on the floor. Near the window are two artist's easels, each holding an unfinished canvas covered with wide swatches of bright colors.

"I didn't know you were a painter, Teresa," I say when she returns to the living room.

"Not I," she says. "Ludwik."

"How many years has he been painting?"

"Since many years," she says. "Since childhood. Always painting, drawing."

"Does he sell his work?"

"Is difficult," Teresa says. "Because not realist. Is, how you say, abstractive. People are not understanding. You are translator, intellectual lady, you understand. Most people not."

"Did he sell in Poland?" I ask.

"In Poland he made works for the government," Teresa says. "Posters, pictures for books, post office stamps. But he wants always to do abstractive. So we come to America, because he said in America is it more possible to make money with abstractive. More intellectual people."

"I see he likes bright colors," I say.

"Colors are for him thoughts," Teresa says. "Flashes in mind like bright colors, one moment, then gone. For him is thought more important than realist world."

"I see," I say. "Well, I hope he'll soon become successful."

"I hope also," Teresa says. "He is working always very hard. I am cleaning in office building every night for buy paint and canvas. Very much cost. We go now, I fix leak."

Frank Schroeder and I go to a cinema near his office. The cinema has a large marquee with the words FRENCH EROTICA in large red letters, and a display window with pictures of girls holding their breasts.

"I go to this kind of theater whenever I need to relax after a day of reading legal documents or fighting it out in a courtroom," Frank Schroeder says.

We sit up front, because Frank Schroeder says that the quality of these films is often poor and we may miss a lot of the details if we sit in the back.

We come in on the opening scene of a film about four students who are unhappy because they have to spend Christmas vacation at their college. In no time at all, the two girls are inviting the two boys to help them decorate their Christmas tree, which is almost finished except for the star at the tip. One of the girls goes up a ladder with the star, while the two boys hold the ladder steady and look up her legs. The rest of the film shows the four of them on the sofa and in the bed, grunting and moaning and pleading.

Another film is about a lonely housewife who takes pity on the young red-haired gardener working outside under the hot sun and invites him in for a glass of lemonade. While he is there, she asks his opinion of the new bed she has just bought. They try it out together.

There is a film about two women playing with each other. The most interesting part of this film is when one of them takes out a long hose. This is what the German philosophers call a Ding an sich. Each woman takes hold of an end and does various things with it.

There are other films. I am the only woman in the theater. Frank Schroeder puts his hand on my leg and gradually unbuttons my skirt. I am wearing one of those skirts that button all the way down the side. Buttonholes are less expensive for clothing manufacturers to do than zippers.

It takes Frank Schroeder awhile to unwind from his day of reading legal documents. He undoes most of the buttons and fumbles with my slip and pantyhose. When he decides it is time for us to leave, he gets up and walks out so fast we have to stand in the back of the theater while I button my skirt.

We go to Frank Schroeder's apartment. He is very excited and keeps going longer than usual. When he falls asleep, I put my clothes on and get into a taxi and go home.

The advantage a woman has when she goes to the man's place is that she can put her clothes on when he is finished and she can go home. When he comes to her place, she has to be polite and let him sleep over if he wants. This was explained to me a few years ago by a woman who was in her sixties and had two husbands in cemeteries, and several lovers.

Work continued relative to the preparation of the 1990 budget for this operacion. In este aspect, it would be wise to establish, clearamente and in accordance con the laws of the country, the legal and labor situation of the personnel hired, with a view to meeting any investigation or demand of the authorities, and the salaries paid to the persons concerned, so that they can be approved as recuverable costs.

"A few of the sentences sound a little strange," the oil-company executive says. "Maybe you could just double-check them. Also, there are a few typos you could correct if you're going to be retyping the translation."

Are you aware that on August fourth, one thousand nine hundred eighty-three, Mr. P.M. confirmed before an attorney that the sale made to Mr. B.E. on August sixth, one thousand nine hundred seventy-seven, had been a sale of six hundred forty one-thousandths of one percent of the petroleum to be produced in the petroleum areas covered by the petroleum contract with the Government of the Republic?

I was not a party to this transaction, and only a judge can rule on it.

Are you aware that on December twenty-ocho, one thousand nine hundred seventy-nine, Mr. P.M. sold to the D. Company, Inc., the same petroleum rights he had sold to Mr. B.E. on August sixth, one thousand nine hundred seventy-seven?

The company must have the relevant documents. It is not

my job to sit in judgment on the actions of Mr. P.M. I am only a translator.

Weekly report.

Newly renovated one-bedroom apartment. Charming building. New kitchen and bathroom appliances and floors. Spacious, elegant luxury.

The bedroom was created by building a small wall. Because of the position of the window, the wall had to be built at an angle.

As we agreed, I am enclosing the report you requested. I hope that this report will meet your needs, and I shall of course be glad to discuter it with you.

A police report about a robbery, translated from the Spanish.

On Thursday morning, at around nine-fifteen, la Señora B.G.R. is in her home. With her are her minor daughter, aged one and a half, her maid, her gardener, and a plumber. The maid opens the front door and goes outside for a few moments to hablar with the gardener, leaving the door open. The telephone rings, and the maid goes back into the casa to answer it, once again leaving the door open. Suddenly she becomes aware of the presencia of an unknown male who is pointing a gun at her.

The unknown male proceeds to overpower her and drag her into the master bedroom of the house. Meanwhile, other armed males are overpowering the plumber, the gardener, and la Señora B.G.R. and her daughter, and are forcing them into the master bedroom. The attackers order the victims to remain silent, and threaten to kill them if they make any moves. The attackers then proceed to ransack the house, making a great deal of noise in the proceso.

Around ten-thirty, the noise stops. Looking out of the bedroom window, la Señora B.G.R. sees her neighbor working en his garden. Opening the window, she calls out to him, telling him what has happened and asking him to call the police. The police arrive at the house several minutes later. The attackers have stolen all the jewelry, cash, and electronic equipment. That is all. Read and signed accordingly.

    Frank Schroeder needs a translation of an interview with an artist who is famous for paintings in which the male and female sexual organs play a major role.

The artist explains his work to the interviewer.

"Principalmente son los órganos sexuales la base del trabajo," he says. "Este es para mi una cosa de sugerencias, de simbolismos en mi arte, que trata de evitar al máximo el realismo, la obviedad."

The sexual organs are the principal bases of my work. For me it is a matter of suggestions, of symbolisms in my art, which endeavors as much as possible to avoid realism and obviousness. I want the sexuality or sensuality in my work to be como suggested, not something overwhelming, obvious, or crude.

The interviewer asks about the reason for this highly sensual symbolism.

"It has been a motivo principal in my work for many years," the artist explains. "There's a great deal of sensualidad y sexualidad in almost all my works, a sensual or sexual constant, but always treated in different ways."

The interviewer asks the artist about the meaning of his work.

"It is the world of relaciones with bodies," the artist says. "It can be sexual, sentimental, or afectiva. Bodies meet, part, receive one another, hurtle against one another, recover."

The interviewer asks about the artist's most recent work, a series of paintings of women.

"I wanted to show different images of Woman," the artist explains. "For example, I wanted to create the image of a girl who is harassed by three men, but ultimately she is the one que chases them. Hay a picture of a virginal girl who comes to earth to love all human beings. And there is a vision of the Feminine as phallic woman, as tabu, the woman who absorbe, possesses, creates problemas."

Frank Schroeder is tieless and jacketless when I arrive at his office with my translation. He has rolled up his shirtsleeves, and his large white arms are visible to the elbows. He puts his feet up on the desk and reads the interview straight through without looking up and without saying anything to me. After a few minutes I leave.

My neighbor has been filling up the metal shelves that she found outside the store. Her collection of wide-brimmed hats takes up two shelves. The other shelves are filled with things she has found in the street.

Her latest treasure is a wire cage that opens on one side. I pick it up and study it.

"What will you use it for?" I ask her.

"Oh, a cage like this can be used for dozens of things," she says. "You'll see."

She is building a collection of plastic dishes and tableware in the same way. She explains her method to me one morning when I am having coffee with her.

"There's nothing to it," she says. "You go into one of those fast-food places and buy a cup of coffee. While you're drinking it, you quietly collect all the used plates and forks and spoons lying on the tables near you. After you've brought them home and washed them, they're just as good as new."

I show her the brochure I am translating for the one hundred seventy-fifth anniversary silver spoons created by a German silverware manufacturer.

"Very nice," my neighbor says, studying the picture of the spoons. "Your work brings you into contact with artistic things. But when it comes to practicality, plastic is the best."

. . .

Weekly report.

One-bedroom plus. Add up the charms of this one-bedroom with new appliances in separate windowed electric kitchen, wide-plank hardwood floors, new tiled bath, extra room that can be used as den or second bedroom.

Classy studio apartment. Spacious, sunny, airy, completely renovated, in full-service building.

"I have a feeling you don't know how to look at apartments," Pauline says. "I really ought to go with you when you go out looking."

"Mr. Saunders want to put elevator in," Teresa says. She is in my kitchen fixing the handle of my refrigerator.

"He wants to put an elevator in this building?" I say.

"Yes. He says too high building for only stairs. He says some person have heart attack and then he have to pay hospital. So he want to put elevator in."

"Where would he put it?" I ask.

"Ludwik say only place is possible is in side space to next-door building, how you call it?"

"You mean in the alleyway between this building and the one next to it?" I say.

"Yes, in there," Teresa says.

"On the outside wall of the building, in other words."

"Yes, going up outside of building."

"Does the city allow outside elevators?" I ask.

"Mr. Saunders say yes, but many permissions necessary. Many papers for city."

"Then he'll be able to raise our rents," I say.

Teresa shrugs. "Everywhere is rent raising," she says.

En application of the provisions of the decree of September thirtieth, nineteen hundred fifty-three, and its modifications subséquentes, the rent shall be increased to one hundred fifteen thousand francs per annum, effective on first January. If the tenant estime abusive la rent increase, il may file an objection, within thirty days after la réception de this notice, with the Landlord-Tenant Conciliation Board.

"You're getting a little careless about your work," Frank Schroeder says.
"Careless about my work?" I say.
"Yes. I'm finding some strange errors in your translations," Frank Schroeder says. "Spelling errors, typos, garbled sentences."
"I see."
"Documents with errors in them aren't accepted by the courts."
"Oh," I say.
"Just thought I'd mention it," Frank Schroeder says.

I am awakened in the middle of the night by a loud crash, followed by rumbling sounds. I go to my window and look, but I see nothing out of the ordinary. I think about my visit to Chichicastenango, the market town in the mountains of Guatemala, and about the earthquake there.
There is no sign of damage to my apartment. My building is not shaking. I go back to bed.
When I take to the street in the morning, I see that two buildings in my street have collapsed, sending heaps of rubble onto the sidewalk and ruining cars parked at the curb.
Work crews are clearing away the rubble and putting up scaffolding over the sidewalk in front of the buildings. A crowd has gathered to watch. I see Teresa and my neighbor in the group. I see Ludwik standing off to one side, sketching the ruins and the people.
"Did you hear the crash?" my neighbor asks.
"Yes," I say. "It woke me up."
"It woke up the entire neighborhood," my neighbor says. "For a minute I thought it was an earthquake."

"Two so strong-looking buildings," Teresa says. "Now ruins like in war."

One of the collapsed buildings is the one that had the mural.

In these old buildings, the brick walls are lined with plaster. This is not the system of the future. The system of the future is drop-in cassette walls that can be changed quickly and easily. It is astonishing to note how we are gradually becoming aware of the consequences of the technological wave in areas that seemingly have nothing to do with it. Technological waves washed over the beachhead of European industry even before the 1970s. Now they are moving us from vertical integration to a solar system of autonomous buildings united by a standardized communications system, from monadic structures to systemic networks, and from single-sector systems of logic and of mono-sectoriality to a systemic vision.

Studio apartment in a good area. Quiet. Terrace. All new fixtures. In an old building that has been rehabilitated and equipped with modern kitchen and bathroom. The studios are all in the rear, facing the walls of the buildings in the next street. The terrace is large enough to hold two chairs.

I tell the real-estate agent I shall call her back.

On the train a man across the aisle keeps staring at me. He is a short, thickish, middle-aged man with hair growing around the edges of his ears and with glittering eyes.

I study the other passengers for a while. I shift to the product advertisements. I realize that the man staring at me is moving his hand up and down under the envelope on his lap.

I saw a man doing this on a train one day when I was a young teenager.

The trains nowadays carry a great deal of product advertising written in other languages. We translators are at a disadvantage when it comes to advertising in foreign languages, and even in English: we see all the mistakes.

Aprenda a hablar inglés ahora en su casa. The picture

shows a set of cassette tapes and a man listening to a tape recorder. La máquina del lenguaje, the ad calls it. The machine of language. The language machine.

A robot could be a language machine. I saw a robot recently in the lobby of an office building. A robot is a computer with the shape of a human body. He is a shiny, iridescent steel creature, about as tall as a woman of average height but with a large head. His blue eyes glow for a few seconds at a time and then dim, and he has a wide mouth with a red light that moves from side to side as he talks. I am saying *he* and *his* because he is a language machine with a man's voice.

He is answering the questions of the people who have gathered around him. After a few minutes, he excuses himself, saying he has to find his transportation module, and glides across the lobby, swiveling his head from side to side in search of the revolving door.

L'ordinateur pourra-t-il devenir plus intélligent que l'homme? Pourra-t-il être doté d'une conscience? Pourra-t-on transférer dans un ordinateur l'intélligence et la conscience d'un homme, le rendant presque immortel puisque indéfiniment réparable?

Can the computer become plus intelligent than human beings? Can it be endowed with self-awareness? Will it be possible to transférer to a computer the intélligence and self-awareness d'un homme, thereby making him indéfiniment réparable and hence quasi-immortal?

With highly perfected silicon chips, thousands of electronique circuits are grouped into an area just slightly larger than half a square centimeter. Chips containing a million circuits devraient être available around nineteen-ninety. At that point the grouping of electronic circuits will be almost as compact as the circuits of the human brain. By around nineteen-ninety-five the growth courbe of the ordinateur should exceed the capacity of the human brain.

"Imagine what it will be like when we have computers that

can really think," Pauline says. "Now you understand how revolutionary all this is. A whole new world is being created, and you and I are part of it."

But the technological revolution goes beyond the computer. It is all a question of systemic integration of information. There has been a shift to the integration of management-information systems and programming. The integration of information systems, the integration of various robbers of information existing in an office, are important goals, and robots are now recognized as a strategic asset. The physical, technical management of information will be integrated with decision-making, planning, general management, budgeting, and the operation itself. If we seize this opportunity to rethink the organization of work, it will be a genuine turning point in the creation of the new world. It is all a matter of integration.

    Weekly report.

Studio, good closets, separate kitchen, microwave, exciting location.

Huge alcove studio, can be converted to one bedroom. Luxury elevator building. Mint condition.

Lovely, livable one-bedroom in elevator building, carpeted halls, small separate kitchen, concierge on duty twenty-four hours a day, all amenities, treed street.

    In application of the dispositions of the decree of thirtieth September, nineteen hundred fifty-three, and of its subsequent modifications, my rent is increased to five hundred dollars per month, beginning next month. If I esteem this rent increase abusive, I may, within thirty days from the date of my receipt of the notice of increase, file objections to the increase. But in this city there are thousands of people waiting to take the places of tenants who file objections to their rent increases.

"It's too much for the slum you're living in," Pauline says. "With a little effort, you could find a better place."

· · ·

I help my neighbor bring home a table that she has found in front of a building to the east of the house.

"A beautiful thing," she says as we are carrying the table through the streets. "I don't understand how people can bear to throw out valuable things like this."

The table is a round black lacquered table with colored-glass floral inlays. We place it in front of the sofa.

My neighbor has been collecting jars, bottles, magazines, and newspapers, which are piled in heaps on the floor. She now has four red plastic chairs around the folding table, and she has hung two sets of automobile tire chains on one wall as a decorative sculpture.

"I found the chains in a garbage pail outside a gas station," she tells me. "I can't imagine why anyone would throw such valuable things away. The minute I looked at them, I knew they'd be perfect as a wall decoration. Modern sophisticated abstract neo-realist art. A perfect foil for this floral coffee table, which is, in fact, folk art."

"How do you manage to carry all these things?" I ask.

"I'm still very strong despite my age, dear," she says, "and I'm able to carry a lot of things. And I never go out without at least one large plastic shopping bag. I remember one day I forgot my bag. The things I saw in the streets that day! Wonderful things I could have used in my apartment. I still feel like crying every time I think about it. That taught me a lesson I've never forgotten. Always take a shopping bag with you when you go out, dear."

My brain and my neighbor's brain are blurred and imprecise brains. The future of the computer depends on making its operation less and less precise and more and more blurred, so that it will come to resemble the human mental processes.

During the week, a preliminary contact is established with the new Deputy Director of Energy. A personal friend of the Minister, Alejandro A., arranges a meeting with the Deputy Director, which is also attended by Messrs. R. and F. The Deputy Director has a very frank and open discussion with the attackers. He states at the inicio that since he has just taken possession of his post, he is not yet thoroughly familiar with all aspects of our activity or the various of contents of operaciones contracts in effecto.

The Minister provides certain ladies with diez dólares para taxi fare, and vouchers for free hairdressing appointments at the Salón de Pedro. Kulturelle acceleration, unequal development, und moralische ambiguity are features of European meetings. The Minister slips dólares into the hand of the new Deputy Director of Energy, who rattles them in his hand, then puts them into his pocket. The previous Deputy Director of Energy used to take them with his fingertips como si they were butterflies. A girl will be coming to my room at nine, the Minister says. I am sorry, Signor, very sorry, the new Deputy Director of Energy says, but we do not accept artists in this hotel. Then he returns the dinero to the Minister, and mentions the names of a few nightclubs and brothels. The Minister nevertheless expresses great interest in our actividades, and feels that the decision to sign the contract with us would be both very logical and very raisonable. He asks for technical information about certain problems that are being discussed at the meeting of the girls. The new Deputy Director for Energy assures us that he is ready to provide every possible assistance with a view to cooperation between his office and our company, and that he will always act para terminar to terminate the Minister.

Complaint from Frank Schroeder, who is returning one of my translations for changes. He is objecting to my translation of a certain word in one of the appellate-court decisions. I read the dictionary definition to him. He does not accept it.

"No, that's wrong," he says. "I don't care what's in your dictionary. Aside from that, there are too many typos. And a lot of the sentences are garbled and don't make sense."

I look at Frank Schroeder's arms, which are large and hairless, with thick wrists and big hands. They look made for fighting or painting, not for converting words. I shall probablement be in his neighborhood again in the near futuro, and we shall then have an oportunidad to talk about his arms, so spacious and luxurious and brilliantly designed without compromise and with revolutionary mécanique, a consequence of the technological wave in my apartamiento, where I sit converting words into a thin network that is rudimentary but is nevertheless organized with modern computerized systems of programming, management, and kontrolle.

Weekly report.

Studio, quiet, in a high-rise building, convenient location. When I arrive at the building, I see a woman sleeping on the steps. Her swollen legs are covered with sores. A dense mat of gray hair is hanging down her back.

A press release from the Ministry of Energy announces that the petróleo company has signed a new contrato with the government. The Minister says that the exploratorio work of the company will total one hundred ten million words. One hundred fifty royalties of seismic robbers will be invested, and three thousand five hundred questions will be opened up. This seems to be the iniciación of a new era of understanding and cooperación for the conversion of words and revolutions.

Looking into the courtyard, I see that the soleil is shining and the sky is bleu. Une femme is lying on the ground. A man dans un white coat is bending über her and is listening with a stethoscope at her chest. There are men in the courtyard, masked men armados with guns. Other men are riding up the murs of the building. I hear les voices of men in the hall.

My neighbor and several men are breaking down my door. They rush into my apartment and apuntan their guns at me.

One of the men is a robot, a shiny, iridescent steel Ding an sich of medio height but with an énorme hard-wired head, blue drop-in eyes that glitzern for a few segundos at a time and dann dim, and a wide mouth with rouge lights that move from side to side. What are you doing here, I pregunta him.

My nabuur orders me to be quiet. She is the person who gibt the orders, while I am the traduisant translator.

I prozessiere the world in an era of integration and systematization of systems and words in a thin and rudimentair network of one hundert forty-two thousand drop-ein lift-auf Whereases that wait at the door that turns and spins and draait and tourne in the waves in my apartment, a door multiplied by eras so that it can keep up with a virginal fálico lawyer whose blue eyes are glitzend and whose ear hairs are waving and who unbuttons my rok and watches me translating in search of the Tur that is spinning and tournant and looking pour the translator who is übersetzend and traduciendo and turning and girando and revolviendo and spinning and traduisant y traduciendo the documentos moving bewältigend programmierend organizzante explaining à Pauline multipliant apuntando suggérant integrando glitzernd ordenando présentant el artista translating übersetzend spinning escuchando watching l'immeuble avec the mural falling revolviendogirando übersetzend bewältigando girandoumdrehendo describiendore volviendosugeriendo turningumdrehendvirevoltando. Q

VICTORIA REDEL

Ruby, Darwin, Eurydice

April again, and this means little Holland.

She did it on her own, planting and planting. When? We never saw her planting, and then comes April, her only two months under and the tulips up. We never guessed there were so many kinds, so many colors; and more than just colors, there were colors off of colors, and edges, scalloped, pronged, squared, wisped, roughed, shredded, smoothed.

Are you looking? Are you standing at the porch window with our father in his business suit? Then you see his eyes scan the lawn as if he thinks he will find her down in a flower bed or high in a waxy cup.

We could not get rid of enough tulips to keep our father from the window.

Every day we went out with scissors, but the tulips were not like dandelions or other weeds, they were like the very blades of grass. By the armful, and then by the cartful, we carried tulips to the woods behind our house. We threw, we dumped, and then because we were afraid our father would see the mound of their bright heads, we got our mother's spade to dig a place to drop the tulips in.

We could not keep up with her tulips.

There were early plantings and then later ones that erupted glossy and striped. And our father, back home now and at the porch window, called the patchwork that glowed in the early evening light a miracle, a miracle that she had sent.

We brought our father in a bulb so that he could see that the tulips were not a miracle but born out of the scaled potato-like bodies that she had stuck one by one under the ground.

. . .

Our father came home with tulips wrapped in florist paper to put in vases and then in bell jars about his bedroom. He said he wanted to sleep in a room with tulips covering every inch of room but could not stand to think of cutting a single stalk from her lawn.

When he was not looking, we cut some more.

Are you still with our father? Do you see then, even after the light has gone and there is only the dark shadowed darkness, that he is still standing?

In the morning, we saw that our father's bed was still made as we had made it, the sheets pulled taut to keep our father safely in.

By mid-April, our father started pointing. "Here is a Chellaston Beauty, those are Magnificents, here is a Ruby, those are Queen of Sheba," our father said.

When our father went off to work, we went into our mother's closet, took a few dresses, and let the men load the rest into the charity truck.

The next April, our father turned from the window.

We looked out to the overblown tulips, the last of their petals ready to unhinge.

When we turned back to our father, he was walking out the door in a seersucker suit.

April again, and this means little Holland.

We are down among the beds. There is always work to be done—cutting down finished blooms, keeping the weeds from choking back a single stalk; in November, there is planting the new varieties, the hybrids we have ordered from overseas. We work at night because we now believe that this is what she did, lifting herself from the side of our father and walking out across the black grass.

By morning, we are back inside, calling our father to the

porch window to see the miracle that she has sent. Our father heads out the door, his arm trailing a cheerful wave.

"Look," we call after him, "there is Candy Stick, Parrot, Bijou, Golden Harvest, Golden Age, Darwin, Eurydice, Plasir, Double Early, Double Late."

From out the porch window, we watch the April sky ball up dark, then open.

Do you see our father bent and running?

He does not see that, with each of his steps—not once does he look back—our lawn begins to fade. **Q**

KATHRYN THOMPSON

PV=nRT

    I assure you, sir, I am not in that percentile.
The questions, sir, were hard to understand.
Awoke to find an insect in my bed, sir, *the nature of which I did not understand.*
Flunked that lab practical, sir, because I could not identify the speared organ; because I could not find, sir, the genital opening of the female crayfish near the third walking leg.
Then I saw it, sir—two halves of a worm—inching away. I named it *Annelida,* for worm—only to see it fly away the order *Lepidoptera.*
I cried home to Mother.
You must tell the headmaster first, dear, that it is a duck, and then that it is a mallard, and afterward, if he should like to hear it, that he wobbles when he walks.
All of my malignancies, sir, grown from innocent moles.
A grandfather dead, sir, at the ripe age of twenty-one.
Sir, I have gotten so small as ten to the minus seven in joules and beyond.
I have learned about ergs, sir.
Negative infinity a quantity I've often contemplated, sir.
A kind of homeostasis, scientifically-speaking, sir.
Time is not there yet.
Well, then, minimax: the minimus of a set of maxima.
Yes, sir, those are the facts.
When I found science, it was beautiful, sir, I must tell you. Suddenly my mind was a flurry of the most extraordinary biological facts; all the mitigating factors of my life came to me, all my questions answered: No wonder pee smells like ammonia. It is! It's NH_3! It is! And here's why H_2O boils fast on a mountain: $PV=nRT$! If I may, sir: why, everything I saw, I knew!
    Those pent-up hands of mine, Doctor! They kept shaking!

My grandfather, sir, is dead.

Phosphenes: The lights you see when you close your eyes real hard.

Lysosomes: organelles that self-consume. Interesting concept, sir. Suicide on the cellular level.

Don't you think?

Sir?

You can check the periodic chart if you don't believe me.

Since epiboly, sir. Since the onset of gastrulation, I knew.

And before! During tetrad formation, crossing over, recombination. Every meiotic division! Every germ layer knew! And throughout lactation.

I am told, sir, that at 3 cm. ossification begins.

Yes, sir! Quite the humanitarian, as well. Hovering over the frog that last afternoon with my scalpel and wits (well, there she was again, snapping and waxing), and first I covered his legs with a paper towel and next I told him, you know, Sir Prufrock, your legs are a delicacy in some circles.

He twitched, Doctor.

He did.

My life passed before me. I cried aloud: Come to me, my love.

So much violence in the laboratory! Something always sitting up! But I returned, sir, here I am.

Once a month, my endometrium sloughs off.

The moment was preceded by a moment of defiant terror and of stillness.

Yes, Doctor, I did.

And when I became a woman for the first time, it was like finding science again.

Oh, Doctor!

Sir?

I do, sir.

No man will marry me.

The chemical name describing a bovine NADP-specific glutamate dehydrogenase contains 500 amino acids.

Thirty-six hundred letters, sir! Who needs *mothers*?

I will keep from pulsing forth, extract all emotion from my autonomic nervous system, swallow all urges and drives, remain imperceptible and contained, execute exquisite control of my adrenal medulla.

I have no left-brain activity, sir, I swear.

No sensation below the belt.

None whatsoever.

My mansion waits for me with its silent butler and a dumbwaiter.

My patio is a scene for raucous suburban laughter.

I can lick at my wine with perfect confidence.

I have skinned a yellow formaldehyde rat. Just peeled him back, two rawhide flaps. I am a scientist.

I am meticulous in expression.

I am fit to operate.

I trust you will put in a killing word when the committee convenes, sir. I trust, sir, that justice will prevail.

I beg you, sir.

Sir, I have already bought the sphygmomanometer.

My beeper, sir, here on my belt, it is digital and glows. **Q**

My Mother Dressing

After my father went kind of crazy and spent his spare time driving around the streets of Avondale looking for the synagogue of his childhood, my mother fell in love with a man named Al Kirschbein. I never met Al Kirschbein, but my mother would talk to me about him while she got dressed up for their dates. She would sit at her dressing table and I would sit on the bed—not on my father's side, but on my mother's—and I would watch my mother getting dressed while we talked.

My mother would sit fat and naked at her dressing table, her freckled skin still glistening from her bath. "He's not exactly handsome," my mother would say, pouring a puddle of body lotion into her hand and smearing it over her big and broken-down breasts. "But he's a big man, a lot bigger than Daddy." She would lift one breast and smear the lotion underneath it, and then she would lift the other breast and smear the lotion underneath that one. She would smooth her palms around her fat and swollen belly, so fat and swollen, it seemed to me, that even I could be living back inside there. "And he carries himself so gracefully for a big man," my mother would say, pouring another puddle of body lotion into her hand, smearing it around her swelling flanks, slicking it around her bulging calves and shins.

And while my mother was smearing and slicking, she would start in on the same old story, how I should not blame her, how I should understand that she got so lonely now that Daddy was acting so crazy. She would say, "You don't blame me, do you?" and I would shake my head and say "No," except that my mouth would feel funny when I said it. My mother would stop smearing the lotion, would look up at me, her eyes moist and hard. "Are you sure?" she would say, and I would always say, "Yes, Mother, I'm sure."

Then my mother would tell me to cream her back. I would look at the bottle of body lotion she was gesturing at me with over the back of her shoulder and I would look at the freckled flesh swelling on her back and I would not want to budge from the bed. I would just stay sitting down on my mother's side of the bed, looking at the flesh swelling on my mother's back. She would say, "Come on, do my back, will you?"

I would pick myself up from the bed and go over to my mother's back—and as I took the bottle of lotion from my mother's hand, a queer kind of tingle would pass through my hands like a warning tingle, like a danger tingle, as though I were going to touch something that could hurt me if I was not careful. But I always smeared the lotion onto my mother's back—and as I creamed and rubbed my mother's skin, my fingers would lose their queer tingling, and I would listen to my mother telling me the sweet things that she said Al Kirschbein was always telling her—how incredibly gorgeous she was and how she was the girl of his dreams. I would try to picture Al Kirschbein's fingers touching my mother's skin, but the only fingers I could picture touching my mother were my own. I would dip my fingers into my mother's soft back and trill them up and down the knobby string of her spine and brush them over her shoulder, and think how Al Kirschbein was right, that my mother really was the girl of someone's dreams.

Whenever my mother told me to hook up her down-to-the-waist brassiere, I would yank and pull the back sides of the brassiere together, trying to hook the tiny metal hooks into the tiny metal eyes. My mother's loose back would well up beneath my fingers, would surge up between the hooks and eyes, and I would have to shove the loose flesh back with the heel of my hand and pull the next hook over and shove and pull and shove and pull until I was free to go sit back down on the bed and watch my mother wiggle and huff herself into her boned and zippered girdle, buckle her stockings into her ribboned garters, and then—at last—pull up the nylon underpants that covered the dark, terrible wedge down there at the bottom of her girdle.

And tell me, what did this have to do with Mr. Al Kirschbein, I always secretly wanted to know.

When my mother was finally dressed in her underwear, she would sit back, shake two cigarettes out of the pack on her dressing table, and offer me one of them. "Don't tell Daddy I let you smoke," my mother would say, and we would sit smoking and talking, she sitting on the turned-around chair at her dressing table and me sitting on her side of the bed, just as though my mother thought we were girl friends sitting smoking and talking, just as though my mother thought we were girl friends sitting and smoking and talking about boys.

"Who walked you home from school today?" my mother would begin.

"Three different ones," I would say.

"Three?" she would say.

"Four," I would say.

"Al Kirschbein says I'm a wonderful person," my mother would say. "Can you imagine what it's like to hear a man like Al Kirschbein saying you're just such a wonderful person after living all these years with your daddy?"

I would watch my mother rummage among the things on the dressing table—the bottles, the vials, the jars, the unguents. She would lean toward her lighted mirror, would spit with a spitting sound onto a cake of black mascara, would scrub a tiny, bead-encrusted brush against the cake, would sweep the brush up her pale eyelashes, would sweep up and up again and again, until her eyelashes turned into black and sooty spikes. She would slap rouge onto her cheeks, would crayon lipstick onto her lips, would suddenly stop all this and, waving the tube of lipstick as if it were a wand, would say, "If your father should decide to turn up for supper, could you heat up the leftover pot roast for him, please?" Spraying perfume from a bulb-topped bottle, spraying perfume behind her ears, under her fat arms, into the crease between her big breasts, my mother would say to me, "Could you please be a sweet dear and do this for your daddy, please?"

Then my mother would say to me to give her a kiss for good luck, and I would kiss my mother and I would tell my mother to have a wonderful, wonderful time with Mr. Kirschbein, and my mother would tell me to have a wonderful, wonderful time with my father—and I would.

But not until I had sat naked at my mother's dressing table and rubbed lotion onto my hands and rubbed the lotion onto my body and listened to my heart—and to the vagrant heart of my mother—beating, beating, beating. Q

Mr. and Mrs. from Missouri

Before Assembly, she was in Maintenance, inspecting the fuel tanks, checking seams, filing clearance reports. She lasted two years in the tanks. If it hadn't been for her partner, George, she would never have lasted that long. Sometimes, when she would get up in there and start crawling around the smooth curved sides, light streaming from the lamp strapped to her head, she would lose all sense of time. Part of it was the fumes. They could never get the tanks pumped out enough to remove the smell of her father's kerosene heater, and she was back in Castroville, Artichoke Capital of the World.

Part of it was just swing shift—three to eleven—not getting home to San Jose until one o'clock in the morning and not getting down to sleep until five or six, when the other women were beginning to toss and roll and wake up. The other part was the muffled sound of hammering from the body shop; it resounded through the tank like ancient tractors stuttering through early morning fog. "Garlic fog," said Papa. It rolled in from the dehydrators in Gilroy, clouding the air. "Makes you hungry," said Papa.

She would feel George's hand tugging at her shoulder—"Cecilia."

She would tell him that she would have to start all over, would have to recheck every seam, and George would say never mind, it was too late. He would tell her to sign the report anyway and that he would scan the tank for her before his shift was over, that she should go out and get some air.

Now that she has switched over to Assembly, she does not want to go back to the tanks. She does not like to think about what a bad half of the team she'd made with George, and she does not want the same thing to happen with Chastain.

She is new on Interior Assembly and just wants to eat her

meal and get back on the line, where Chastain is teaching her the difference between what is in the manual and how to put aircraft seats together. "No matter what happens," he tells her, "they should not disconnect from the main body."

Sometimes she likes them. This one wears his hair long and pulled back in a rubber band. He is big-boned and tall and doesn't shave.

"Break's almost up," he says. She smiles at him. She does it because they are going to be together a long time.

But Chastain does not get up from his place. "I need to tell you what happened during Vietnam," he says, staring into his coffee. "I think I can tell you."

She does not say anything except, "How long is it?"

"I can break it up. Give you a little at a time."

"*Pues.* Okay. Shoot."

It takes a long time. It takes days.

The Performance Partner Plan was something Corporate came up with about three years ago. Cecilia was living near the airport then, working on a plan to start her own document delivery service with Autumn. But they couldn't get Venture Capital to float them, so it didn't work out.

Cecilia applied for a job in Maintenance and was hired, because she had once worked for an airline and was already Union. She was just in time for the kickoff of Performance Partners, and because she was a double minority, she was written up in the company organ. She and George attended a couple of Quality Circles, read the manual, and decided that it was nothing but watching each other work and giving constructive criticism, which is how they would have worked anyway. Sometimes they would fill out a report, suggesting a lefthand approach instead of a righthand entry, but other than that, it never changed their life.

She jogs in place at the corner, waiting for the light to change. Across the street, Autumn steps up into the bus.

The doors hiss as they close behind Autumn. Cecilia wishes she had worn her bra. She wishes her breasts were small like Autumn's.

The park is almost empty—all the normals are at work, except for the old ones and dogs. She circles the pond twice. A man wrapped in a blanket on a bench watches her breasts as she passes. Both times, he calls to her in Spanish, but she pretends not to understand. She does not want to talk to anyone. All she wants to do is go home and sleep and go to work and put things together.

"I was a Senior," says Chastain, handing her an extra napkin. "And I was in Pershing Rifles, already set for a commission."

She nods, as this seems important to him. She cannot eat her enchilada—it is not like what Mother used to make.

The cadets had Close-Order Drill or Small Unit Tactics twice a week after classes, in an open meadow behind the gym. That afternoon, it was already raining. Chastain could hear distant thunder like far-off mortar fire. Sergeant Brown was positioning the men in the meadow to practice combat formations. Chastain was a squad leader and it was his responsibility to take care of his men. He told Sergeant Brown that he was worried about the storm, sending his men out into an open field like that. "Brown said, 'Listen, Chastain, when you get out in the jungle, you're not going to be worrying about a little rain.' " He said if Chastain was so eager to protect his men, he could just get his butt up there to the top of the hill under that old manzanita tree.

"I can guess how the story ends."

"I have to do this my own way," Chastain says. But he stops talking and finishes his meal.

They start riding home together after the shift. Chastain takes her as far as his turnoff to Milpitas, and she takes

BART the rest of the way. Sometimes, Chastain tells her, he goes to the all-night movie or to a bar after work. Sometimes, he says, he picks up a twelve-pack for home. It helps him sleep.

One of the Performance Partner ideas they turn in receives some kind of prize for The Best Suggestion of the Month: Do the same thing at the same time, but on opposite sides. They have their picture taken for the house organ. Management is in the picture too, shaking Chastain's hand. In the picture, Management has his arm around Cecilia's shoulders.

"I wish I could see you with your hair all down," says Chastain. He was buying her doughnuts at the twenty-four-hour store.

"Finish the story," she says.

Chastain didn't know what hit him. The other men said it hit the tree first, blasting it straight down the middle and running to ground. Sergeant Brown was staring down at him, they said, cursing Chastain so fiercely they could hardly get permission to move the body across the parade ground to the infirmary.

"All I know is I was standing in a green field with straight rows of some kind of vegetable. There were people stooped over harvesting the crop—men, women, kids, people. When they straightened up, I saw they were all waving and smiling at me. It was like I was an old friend, you know, coming home."

"I belong to this club," she says. "We act out our fantasies, a different fantasy each month. Sometimes we're from outer space. Sometimes we're harem girls, and we all belong to one person."

Chastain looks hurt and puts down his doughnut. "I didn't think you'd make fun of me," he says.

Cecilia, angry, "What I have just told you is private. I never tell anyone outside about the club. If I tell you, it might be because I think it will help you to know that other people do it, too. Think about it."

. . .

Somewhere a bell is pealing, like the one at the Mission. The people in the fields straighten up, turn toward the sound, put down their hoes and rakes, smile. They motion her to follow them toward the sound of the ringing bell. Slowly the people begin to fade, until all she can see are their smiles.

She gropes for the receiver.

Chastain.

"Do you know what time it is?"

"Ten A.M."

"I was sleeping."

She can hear him exhaling. "We could pick up a twelve-pack after the shift. We could drink it in Milpitas," he says.

They are eating at a table with the others on their team. Franck and Lisa and Theo and Ng Li. Everyone wants to go out after the shift. No one wants to go home. "You coming?" says Theo.

"She has a date," says Chastain.

She does not know when she started talking about her past. All she knows is that it is five o'clock in the morning and she is sitting in a chair in Milpitas, eating fried-chicken wings and drinking beer from the twenty-four-hour store. Chastain sits in front of her yoga-style on the floor, listening. When he is not listening, he is picking out soft runs on his guitar. "You sure know a lot about artichokes," he says.

Autumn takes Sunday off from studying. The two of them pretend they are summer tourists taking the cable car down to the Wharf. They hold hands and stroll past the open-air seafood stalls, drinking wine coolers through straws.

"George is in the hospital," Cecilia says to Autumn, as they look out toward Alcatraz. "You remember George?"

Is Autumn really listening?

She is sleepy and lovely in wine-colored leotards, apple-green pants.

Cecilia breathes deeply, filling her chest with air. George inhaled something in the tank. He stayed in there too long, everybody says.

She catches Autumn's chin and gives her a certain kind of kiss, shocking Mr. and Mrs. Harrison from Missouri. Mr. Harrison will long regret that he has just used up the last snapshot on Mrs. Harrison eating a squid. Back in Missouri, or really anywhere else, telling is not as good as showing. **Q**

ELEANOR ALPER

We Started with Childcraft

At first we only touched above the waist. One of them read a poem out loud while the other one touched you.

Myrna said anything was all right if you were learning. She said her mother said that. She said her mother had a lot of books.

How long it was your turn to be touched was as long as the poem. We closed our eyes while we were being touched. Myrna had the softest hands; her nails were filed and buffed. Lois had hangnails, but you never got tired of being touched by her the way you sometimes did with Myrna.

Lois made flowers in the palms of your hands and drew ivy that twined up and under your arms. She did snakes on your shoulders and faces all over your back. Lois got better at making you feel the difference between her flowers and her faces. The time came when you could feel just which flower she was doing or whether her faces were smiling faces or were sad.

Myrna did mostly stripes and plaids. She worked all over your back and your arms, but she never touched your palms. But it was Myrna who thought of the ice cubes—which is how we began to go below the waist, you know, following the path of the melting ice down into the crack.

Me, I did words, sometimes the words in the poems, or our names in pig Latin. I did triangles, circles, and stars, making the Star of David the most around their ears, since Lois and Myrna were Jewish. Lois made me crosses on my cheeks.

You picked your poem by opening up to a page. If the poem you chose was short the one who was doing the reading might take pity on you and read very slowly so your turn would last longer. Most of the poems were less than a page, but some went on. We started with "Childcraft" and then used Myrna's mother's poems, which were all about love.

Lois got goose bumps on her arms, and her bones stuck out more than Myrna's. But Lois sat perfectly still and never shook or got ticklish the way Myrna did, even with the ice. Myrna was blonde and had fine golden hairs on her arms and had perfectly smooth legs. Lois was dark and had dry skin with scales, but her skin was cool even on the hottest of days. Myrna wore halters. Lois, like me, wore polo shirts.

After Myrna moved, Lois and I had no one to read to us—except each other. We did it then at Lois's house, on the studio couch of her sunporch. It was always damp and cold there. I do not remember there being any sun.

We covered ourselves with a quilt and kept on our clothes and our socks. We lay side by side on our backs, facing one another, our heads up on little piles of throw pillows.

After we grew hips and breasts we filled up that couch and had to lie on our sides, either face to face, or back to back, or face to back—or however it was we could.

And the poems, I'm not sure when it was, but one day we stopped reading them at all. And this was either before or after we had stopped wearing our clothes, which must have been long after we were even bothering to do the flowers or the words—when we both began to just do it up and down and back and forth, starting, though, as we always did, with the toes, and then doing whatever we could reach. **Q**

KATHERINE ARNOLDI

Canton, Ohio: 1956

The shed is next to the house I am supposed to go to. It is the house where a woman sits with a handkerchief to her nose, where a grown-up sleeps with her knees up in the bed next to me, where a boy sleeps in the bed with me. We just came to this house from someplace I do not remember.

At night I sit on the floor, mash soda crackers into a bowl, then lick them out with my tongue. The boy who sleeps in the bed with me puts his head on the floor against a wall, then pushes his legs up and wobbles there, hanging by his heels in the middle of the wallpaper. The grown-up bangs the screen door against the house, gets in a car. The chair where the woman sat opening and closing and folding and tearing a handkerchief is empty. I want to see my eggs, just to look.

There are three eggs. If I pick one up, my hand is sandy inside all day, a special hand.

Behind the house I am supposed to go to is an alley and children play there. They hold to the edges of a blanket, then wave it up and down until someone jumps inside. They fold dolls into cloths, then lay them in cardboard boxes. The boy who sleeps in the bed with me chases boys who have sticks for guns, baseballs, bats.

At night, I see the eggs on the roof falling off.

The woman sitting in the chair with the handkerchief to her nose is not my mother.

The eggs are stuck inside a bowl of twigs and feathers and gum wrappers, and a finger of the roof curls up, brown, around it.

When the girls in the alley notice me, they coo over me, pat my head, then put their fingers on their braids.

The grown-up leads me out onto the back porch and puts

me down between her legs on the step in front of her. She rubs oil on my head and tells me her secret.

The sky is white.

I climb the ladder, rest my stomach on the top rung and pet the eggs. I pick them up with two fingers, tuck them into my pocket, then inch down. I hold my dress up with the eggs in it, in the pocket, and skip to the house to show everybody inside. But someone pulls the pocket open, looks in, puts my arms in the air, pulls my dress off, throws it in the tub, turns on the water. The dress puffs up, blue in the water. I get the pieces of the shell on my finger, put them in my mouth, and swallow them all. **Q**

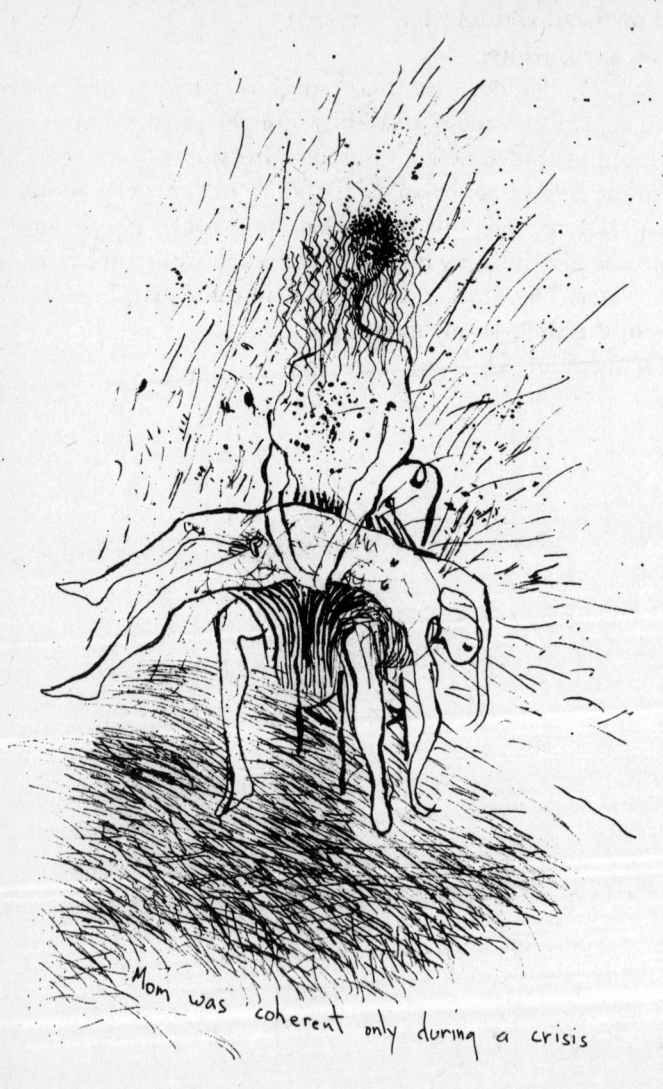

SUSAN RAWLINS

Farewell, Silver—Goodbye, Scout

I'm sneaking out late at night
to untie all the horses.
If they escape,
then no one can try
to ride to the rescue
of those who tie themselves
up, lie down
on the railroad tracks,
and send for the train.

SUSAN RAWLINS

Equity

Gordon Jackson is dead, who was Hudson
to most people, upstairs and down,
but whom I knew as the music master
who wanted to marry Miss Brodie.

Shot by the shooting party. One of
the Scots who also heard no tunes
of glory. Not the second lead, even,
but always leader of the followers.
How will Roger Bartlett escape
without his right-hand man?

Arthur Kennedy dead. Anthony Quayle,
knighted at last, dead. Whom nobody
noticed in *Lawrence*—oh, yeah, what's
his name, *him*. Killing the whole cast,
Quinn and Guinness already at risk.
The unknown Egyptian with five lines,
Ghitan of Aleppo.

Astaire was always a star—never
a world without him. Cary Grant,
Bette Davis, asking for it, enormous,
shining, letting it show. How
could we keep them? Olivier
tottering one grand decade
to his theatrical grave.

You'd think you'd be safe with
Selma Diamond. *(Who?)* That
middle-aged bit player's rasp

at the switchboard: "I'm sor-ry.
This hotel does not provide
such a service." Few noticed,
fewer cared. "And not behind
no pillars nor posts." How
could she die?

Gordon Jackson is dead. It does
no good to be loyal and true,
unnoticed, essential, and good.
All those years of low, steady light.
Doomed, like De Niro, before
he became important. *(It is
not my caring that kills them,*

that risk.)
Expect the imminent death of
Robert Stephens. *(Never mind.)*
It does no good to be life-sized,
a little smaller. It does no good,
after all, to keep your head down.

SUSAN RAWLINS

If This Goes On

He has promised he won't start
to grieve for the carrots, waving
their frondy things in the breezes,
eager to live out their vegetable

lives. But animals, yes. Animal products.
I don't dare ask as he heads out the door
with his tool belt what he's seeing reflected
in one-by-six and quarter-inch ply.

Animals. Animals, vegetables.
He says he's not giving up meat, but
some things look too much like what they
are. And he's had so much trouble with

his own back—bone spurs, compression,
the tenth thoracic, thinning jelly.
So the oxtail stew, if tasty, was
uncomfortable—animal, vegetable,

mineral rights—
sadly picking out gristly parts,
saying, "That's a disk."
"That's a disk."

SUZANNE PAOLA

Lazarus

No night seems quiet after that sleep.
Martha, Mary, it's pointless to ask where I've been.

Only know the morning was unendurable as it
    touched your hair.
And that for three days my body left me alone.

Can you accept me, with your pitchers of wine;
can you accept me, one of the many

dead, all scented and wrapped and sealed,
beyond your deepest visions of what I am.

I didn't know which death to expect—
His of the loving father and the word,

or the Roman one, with its black waters,
or the body wandering back to me in its ignorance,

or nothing.
I didn't know when I rose what I was going to,

whose voice called my name,
and the light—simply my sister's torch.

Lord, rescue me from having been.
This world is a mote in your eye:

the platter of meat they offered me, and the wine,
the tallith they threw on my shoulders,

the feeling of hands.
Lord, rescue me from having been.

Mud pouring in slow tongues from cut fields,
the renunciatory flights of birds;

I had left everything without me, and it lived;
I was the gold poured

in the shape of a calf, too heavy for heaven,
too idolatrous for the world.

See the cowled leper at the edge of the crowd—
I've seen his face in clear water

though everyone told me not to look:
the mouth a gash, nose like the knuckle of a thumb,

and something pulled inside me;
to his church am I moved—

Don't cry, Martha; I am not spring, though I come
renewed from the earth,

and I am not summer, though the vulture swarms
reel in wonder at my breath;

I am fall, when lake hens nest against the frozen
    edge,
and all the glamour of heaven glows in the ice.

MICHELLE RHEA

Vers Librist

I can get a poem
out of anything
no matter what
it's stuck in.

MARJORIE MILLIGAN

Coats Field, Pay Day

Bernadette in the Grotto stood about a foot and a half tall, most of that being grotto. The stones, at least, were pretty realistic, until she let the kids paint them brown with Rust-Oleum. She decided a face that had seen God was really better left alone.

He learned about layaway, a nickel a week, and you could bring a saint home. Ruby wanted new flooring instead, but he went to the hotel and unlocked the door. The woman wore lingerie like a machine gun and the corn dogs tasted like hell, but, he thought, it is the only pleasure I have.

KIM BRIDGFORD

Cancer

When she was a girl,
She would stand and look out
Over her father's cornfields.
All that rustling growth.
Her mind would hurt,
Trying to think of so much corn.
That's what cancer's like.

KIM BRIDGFORD

Miracles

I

She remembers the day
In fourth grade when she asked God
To change her paper doll
Into a person.
She'd spent a lot of time
On the long blond hair,
The bow lips.
The checkered skirt and blouse.
This doll would not need
The clothes with little white tabs
Because soon those two-dimensional makeshifts
Would fall off smooth shoulders,
The tiny, perfect back.
She would be able to show everybody
God's miracle, and Christianity
Would be as obvious as weather
Or the planets her teacher pointed out
With the crisp fortitude of perfect knowledge
On the map pulled down across the board.
But days passed, and the paper doll
Stayed flat and uninteresting.
Since her clothes were a part of her body,
She couldn't become anything else.

I I

These days, as her headaches wind
Around her brain like a scarf of taut stars,
She sometimes thinks of that time
When she had the audacity
To ask God for a mail-order person of choice.

PLEASE SEND COUPON

AND PAYMENT INFORMATION TO:

THE QUARTERLY

SUBSCRIPTION DEPARTMENT

VINTAGE BOOKS

TWENTY-EIGHTH FLOOR

201 EAST 50TH STREET

NEW YORK, NY 10022

See last page to order back numbers.

Herewith payment or credit card information for the next four issues of *The Quarterly*.

Name_____

Address_____

City_____ State_____ Zip_____

____ Enclosed is my check or money order for $40.00 ($54.00 in Canada), made out to Random House, Inc.

____ Please charge my account with

American Express____ MasterCard____ Visa____

Account # ☐☐☐☐☐☐☐☐☐☐☐☐☐☐☐☐

Signature_____ Exp. ____/____
                                                                             mo. yr.

Inasmuch as *The Q* appears every three months—namely, March, June, September, December—please be patient for your subscription to begin.

Even then she learned the human lessons:
Patience and endurance.
Now, reposing in her saggy flesh,
She feels the results of practice.
Her husband is dead,
And her son has a hard heart.
When she calls him, he won't speak
But lets the telephone silence
Dangle between them.
Yet she waits with the humility
Of a believer, picturing
Faith traveling through her son's body,
Loosening the bits of hatred
Until his heart is one clean place.
Then surely, she thinks,
His voice will bubble up,
Shy, rusty, and penitent,
And say something.

KIM BRIDGFORD

Persephone

At first I was frightened
When the earth opened
And Hades drew me into the darkness.
I knew what could happen
To a girl out walking alone,
Picking flowers.

But I got used to that secret place.
I liked it in the dark,
Where touch was velvety
And sight was smoke and ash,
A dizzy lushness I could not get enough of.

Meanwhile, my mother punished
Everybody else for her own loneliness.
She did not like my father
Promising me to Hades behind her back.
After a while, Father could not stand it,
So he sent Hermes down to get me.

Already Hades and I
Were reading each other's mind:
He handed me a pomegranate,
Aware of my hunger.
He knew that I would not forget
The acid taste on my tongue.

And so every year
I live with my husband for four months;
The other eight I spend
Sick for him, my head thick

With the days I try to sleep away.
My mother believes
I will learn to forgive her,
But I am simple with desire.

Every night I tell her *no, no, no,*
Thinking all the while
Of my body moving
Into the darkness
To say *yes.*

KIM BRIDGFORD

Sister

There's a vagueness to my life
That pulls across my forehead—
Mornings especially—
Like a line of puckered stitches.
Do you know what it's like
To stand at the edge of water
And not know where to look?
That's the feeling I wake to.

Until last week I took care
Of my sister—frail as a plant
On a windowsill
Before a drawn shade.
Her tastes ran to delicate things—
Moths, blown glass, a garnet on a chain.
Each day she'd lie on her bed pillows
And embroider worlds from literature;
She always made me guess the book.
"Don't cook me anything spicy,"
She'd say. "I can't bear that."
By the end she was living on
Sweetened tea, toast
With the crusts cut off,
Soup, bread pudding—
Anything bland.

Some days we would take
Black tabs and glue
And put our family pictures in albums;
Father was so faint
We could hardly remember him,

A man who sold things nobody wanted.
Mother was different,
Taking care of everything,
Until one day she fell down the cellar steps and
    died
Because no one knew where she was.

That left Sister to me.
Who would leave family to strangers?
Especially Sister, like a thin satin ribbon
That needs someone to smooth it out.

But right before my sister died,
I saw a look I had never seen.
You'd almost say wicked,
If you didn't know Sister.
"I just want you to know
I chose this," she said.
"What?" I said, holding her tray;
Dizzy, I sat down.
"I never was sick a day in my life,"
She said, and by the time
I could answer, by the time
I fully understood,
She had turned away from me
And chosen death.

VICTORIA REDEL

Third Month

At first you were in the mouth,
nausea uncalmable.
Or you were the hard
stools of constipation.
At night rocked
over to sleep at a child's hour,
I slept with pillows layered
to ease my swollen breasts.
In books they claimed you were
no bigger than a fingernail,
but I could feel you, gargantuan,
settling in my body, assuming
what you needed to live,
risking everything,
even if it meant risking
mother love.

VICTORIA REDEL

Ninth Month

Already you are moving down.

Already your floating head
is engaged in the inlet
from where you will head out.

Already the world, the world.

Slipping down,
away from my heart.

LYNNE H. DECOURCY

The Life of the Writer

You should see me
with this paring knife,
dividing grapefruit sections.
But surely it is good
to make breakfast
even when it means the fruit
gets cut in half and then
divided with an inadequate tool
into tiny separate sections,
each cut leaving some behind,
the rest spooned out and
gone, before I can even picture the whole
yellow-pink roundness forming
like a small early sun
in silent, fragrant air, gathering into itself
a full measure of juice, somewhere
in a distant orchard long before
it was divided and divided
and divided.

ANSIE BAIRD

New Year's Day, 1990

We met again at the street where the heart resides,
Rue Git la Coeur, near the butcher of small birds,
Near the stalls where rabbits hang head down
In adorable fur coats, near the ice beds
Where giant fish glitter and stare
    from their impassive eyes.
We met in a small dive, La Grenouille,
    green and lively
Like a leaping frog, but we did not dance,
We did not order frog. You arrived
In your brown waterproof coat, hood up,
Although it never rained that week in Paris,
And no other man covered his head.
Perhaps you were a monk disguised as my husband.
Perhaps you were my husband
    disguised as a stranger.
It is the start of a new decade, you said.
I'll be going away, you said.
    This is no kind of a life.
What could I reply? I keep a fierce cat
Concealed beneath my cape. She claws at my heart.
Bite by bite she eats me alive.

MARY LEADER

A Coastal Story

My heart is not in her room!
Look—her bed is made up, and she is gone.

From the attic window, I spot her
at dawn, at sea,
a delicate skiff, journeyed by wind, upon a
    dissolving
surface.

      She left a note:
      I love him, I love him, that's all.

      A girl so used to
      her chin in her hand, her studious lamp.

Oh no, what happens next, what happens next?
I don't know!

        And neither—goddamn him—does he.

MARY LEADER

Among Things Held at Arm's Length

It could be 1932. The branch, for example, could
    be cedar.
They planted cedars around the farmhouses in
    those days.
Hereabouts they did, anyway. Cedars are fast
    growers
and they mass, they're thick. Windbreak, safekeep,
    homeplace.

So when a thunderstorm would rant and rave and
    upchuck itself,
the cedars would take it, would wrestle the thing,
    stop it
at the windows. The people would be lying there a
    yard away
in nice dry bedclothes. The dog's eyes would be
    open, waiting.

And in the afternoon, which is the calm, why then
    the cedars
would shift a little in the breeze and their shadows
would move all dapply on the windows, on the
    white windowsills.
And this is a permanent thing, seen from cradles,
    seen from deathbeds.

The branch could be cedar; the bird could be a
    female cardinal.
I could be my grandmother. Or not. It doesn't
    matter.

It's just that she, for example, whose name was
 Muriel, did have
her window, her branch, her bird, her hour for the
 watch.

MARY LEADER

Trimmed with Eyelet Lace

Mother thinks I'm stupid to iron my nightgowns.
She says, "Didn't you ever hear of wash-and-wear?"
She says, "Who's going to see you in your
    nightgown?"
She says, "Why don't you just sleep in your
    undies—
be cheaper." But she can't say much, seeing as how
I buy my own clothes. I work down at the
    Democrat—
help get the paper out on Wednesday nights,
plus I grade algebra papers for Mr. Cartmell.
His wife works at the phone company.
I wonder what she is like.
One time when I was in the Style Shoppe, I saw
    her
buying a nightgown—one of those nylon ones.
I like cotton a lot better. It feels nice.

MARY LEADER

Middle Daughter's Song

    I look down on you, Town. I can't prove
that the units you use to bind time are wrong:
    the loaf, the nap, the coin.
When I look up, though, the whole sky scoops!
    Safehold my nine aunts, who are sewing,
my father, storekeeping . . . Sundust on the till.
    Your edge is my hope. I am going.

JOAN KINCAID

Brochure

Intimacy in the foreground
at the edge foreplay
blue women and men
                       making it
where the light fails
the fat woman
                doesn't read
her kid stuffing
the fawn in its mouth
ensures con-
              tinued crossing
cars careen
         loveless
overlooks.

JOAN KINCAID

The Birds

Hiding the idea
of themselves

a day this way

austere stratagem

perching in
dark acceptance.

SARAH RANDOLPH

The Iranian

To arouse me, he held a computer in his palm, pointing out the insect legs, the hard black body. I thought he would put it in my mouth. Through several dates he was courtly, touching only my elbow, until one night I kissed his closed lips and his hands moved directly to my breasts. Minutes later, his body, stripped of its tailored synthetic clothes, arched high over mine, as if he practiced a difficult position in the Kama Sutra of Engineers, *The High Tension Bridge,* where the lovers touch only at the genitals.

SARAH RANDOLPH

Movie Dogs

Fashion
is a kind of hope against the present moment.
Lie in the sun, dogs;
in a green suede outfit the future
seems as easy as the cinematic
scene between the scenes at the Cosmo Bar.
Not much about the world makes sense
to us, dogs in the sun,
black dogs
in short black haircuts,
looking at fashion photos.
Boys humping each other in the square,
going over their scripts,
intimate and opaque,
a bad influence.

CAROL LEE

When Ricky Came Home to Lucy

Life was different.
Mom was Mom.
Dad had a job.
Uncle Milty made them laugh
on Tuesdays.

Girls wore dresses,
braided their hair.

Pictures were black-and-white.

Families had one car.
Ours was a Buick.
It had those holes on the side.

That's how it was.

It was not a lifestyle.

CAROL LEE

In Heaven

Where the drapes are closed,
Miss Post cleans her plate.
Licks her lips.
Wrinkles her napkin.
Rests her elbows.

GAIL WRONSKY

Parting, after Desnos

My ugly new love
lost his first wife in the
bathtub, now I'm going
blind. I can imagine
only the distances:

an Archangel
tickles my shoulder with flame.
In another few years
he will ask for my
phone number.

Ask what you like.
What I like is
simply the notion of parting
at death, of seeing in darkness,
of wearing an after-life
dress and escaping
forgiveness.

I'll recover
if you point to me forever and
whisper *Cadaver.* Of course,
that's not vision. I lie
like a sunbeam

amazed
at the edge of the page.

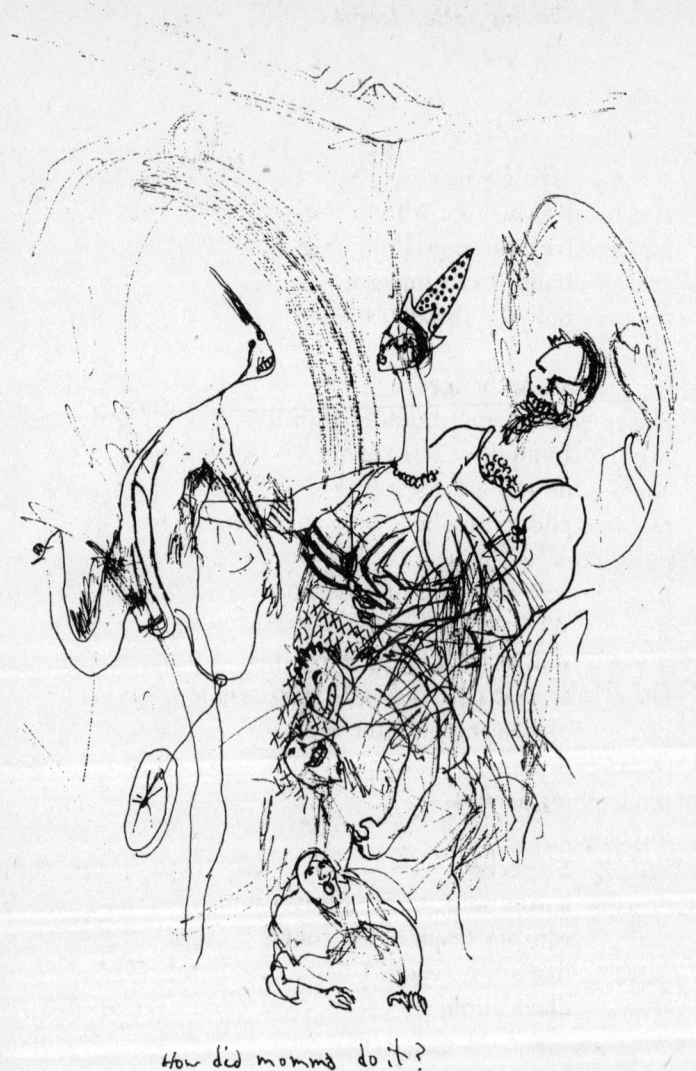

How did mommy do it?

Going downtown to my aerobics class here very shortly. It's a neat class. There's something vital about jumping around with a lot of other people, mostly women, to percussive music. My favorite one is "Wild Thing." People really need to do this. I think it's an essential part of the psyche, jumping around. The instructors are all these very slim women who have a peculiar way of yelling out the commands to do things, which is not expressible in saying things like "Excellent work! Excellent!" which is supposed to encourage you to fling yourself into the jumping around, I guess. There's the sixty-five-year-old lady next to me that keeps up with the whole hour. I have to slack off and go pant for a few minutes over by the rowing machine, and then come back and try again. But she doesn't miss a lick. She's about four feet eleven and slightly pudding-shaped. But she just goes right on without a hitch. Also, this place is up on a second floor, and the big tall windows look out onto Main Street, and there's this guy who owns the sporting-goods store across the street; well, he's a fundamentalist of some kind, and he has been complaining to the City Fathers, whoever they are, that all this bouncing female flesh to be seen in the windows of Adrenaline Plus is obscene and disgusting, or whatever. Anyway, he's been agitating to take Sharon's business license away! I ask you! And there he is over there with all that pointy hard stuff—like skinning knives and rifles with telescopes and Jungle Jim camouflage outfits, for going around killing things and murdering small animals! I mean, this guy will sell you a big 12-gauge under-and-over to go blow away mama deer with big liquid appealing Bambi eyes and he's getting all shirty about all these healthy live females leaping around to "Wild Thing"! Well, the teenagers were here for Thanksgiving—James Harold came up from Houston (that's Jim's nephew), and my nephew Matt came up from St. Louis, and Jim's beautiful daughter came up from southwest Missouri. They were all meeting each other for the first time. Jim and I wanted to get our two families together. We planned activities and menus and the entire Thanksgiving dinner down to the last cranberry. But, as it turned out, teenagers are mostly interested in other teenagers, and another couple here in town that we are friends with have this utterly blond teenage Melissa, and Melissa came over and introduced our teenagers to all of her teenagers and we hardly ever saw any of them, except when they came back in great gangs to have long, complicated parties at our place, and drink up all our beer. Jim and I just left the house and went over to baby-sit Melissa's parents and drink up all their beer. And so it all worked out. Jim's daughter charmed everybody and apparently acquired a new Canadian boyfriend, and my nephew fell in love with Melissa and etc., etc. God, I forgot what it was like being a teenager! It's just one long chorus of "Wild Thing." We took them up to Ainsworth Hot Springs. Did I ever tell you about that place? It's out of a movie set for *Willow*. It's this cave on the side of a mountain full of hot water up to your waist and lights back in there, stalactites and mites, hot pools and cold pools. We go up there as often as we can and steam ourselves, Jim and me. The kids liked it. Then we had to take them all back to the airport in Spokane in two different lots—and while we were down there, we bought a lot of groceries, etc., at a discount place that had security guards. Then you have to smuggle this shit back across the border without paying duty. I bought two ladies' suits because they were about a third of the normal ticket, and then, to smuggle them across the border, I wore both of them. Smuggling is fun! It's the great Canadian pastime. Anyway, it's kind of gloomy here. Low skies. But, hell, I've got my suits. **Q**

HEATHER KEE *to Q*

The Hat

THE QUARTERLY

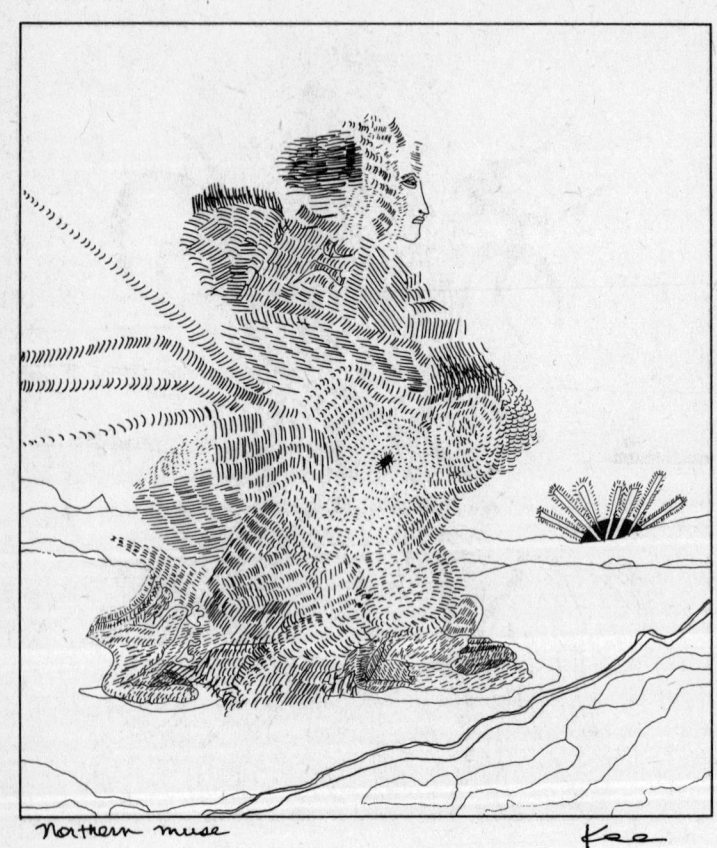

Northern muse

HEATHER KEE *to* Q

The Gathering of Wisdom — Kee

THE QUARTERLY

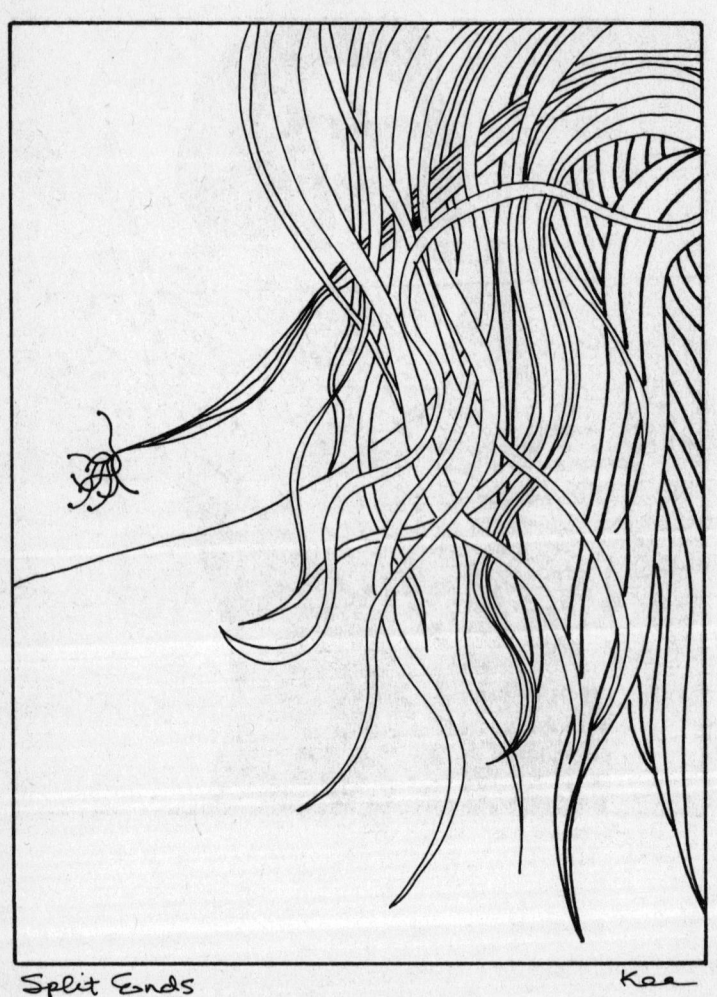

Split Ends   Kee

HEATHER KEE *to Q*

Quest — Kee

THE QUARTERLY

Man on his way to work

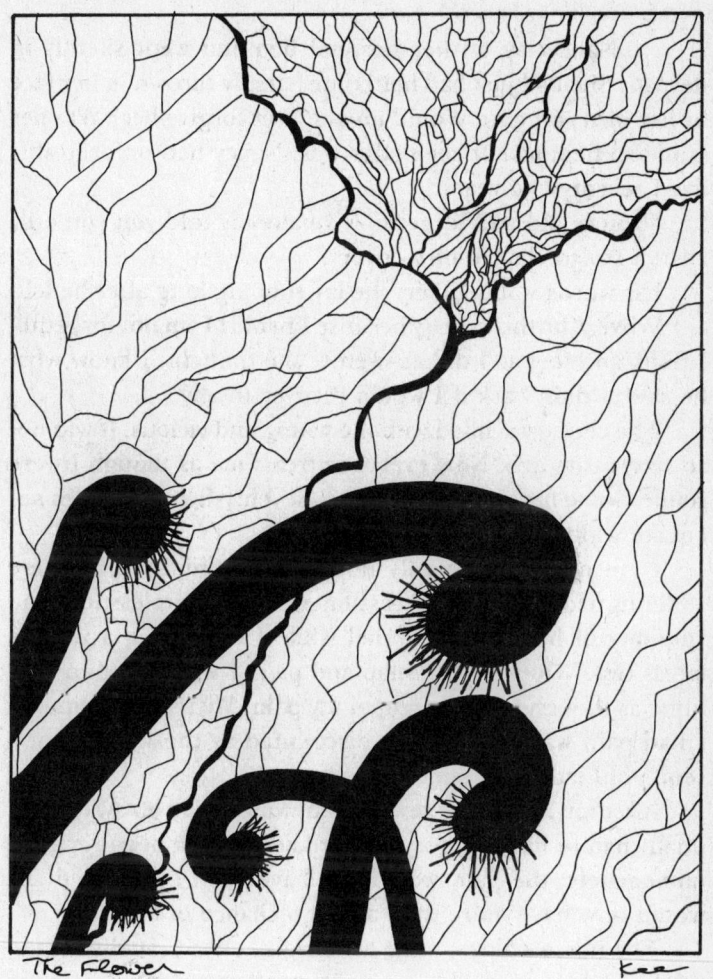

Nancy lay on her hospital bed and wept silently in despair. She had just had her crime harshly thrown in her face by her own surgeon. Would no one ever forgive her? Was her crime so heinous? It seemed it was. Nancy had unforgivably lived seventy-five years.

"You're old and forgetful. I've already told you you only have a 50/50 chance of recovery."

His words stabbed her; she lay sobbing long after he left. Why? Why this cruelty because I'm old? I am not forgetful. I think and feel as I did at twenty, she thought. I know what he said; I didn't ask if I would recover totally.

The country is filled with the young and vicious. It was not so sixty years ago. Now everyone treats me as though I were senile. Some have even told me so. Seventy-five years does not equate with senility.

I am neither physically nor mentally infirm; I am here suffering from surgery necessitated by the carelessness and stupidity of hospital personnel while I was taking a routine stress test. When I felt a snap and pain, I was forced to continue as though I had imagined my pain. My telling them that I had pain was immediately discounted as the whining of a senile old lady, she remembered.

After ten months of severe pain, which "will go away," she finally had to have surgery on her knee. Had it been repaired immediately, the pain would not have been severe and she would now have more than a 50/50 chance of recovery.

The nurse's aides, none too bright, talked cruelly to her, thinking she was unable to understand them. They were in command; she was their idiot subject. It was terrifying that she was under their control. She withstood their insults, attributing it deservedly to their lack of intelligence, but her own doctor, whom she liked and trusted, had crushed her this morning with his attack, which was totally unwarranted.

When had all this begun? she wondered. When did I change to a quivering mass of stupidity?

She thought of her life. She had been assistant to the president of a large corporation until her daughter was born, at which time she resigned. It was customary then for women to resign and care for their children unless there were dire necessities which forced them to continue working. This happened rarely at the level of executives, however. Their salaries permitted planning.

Besides devoting her life to her family—her husband, her daughter, her mother and brothers, she also worked part-time at home. She taught music and painted. While her daughter was in college, she worked half days as a counselor before counseling was a profession. Her major in college was psychology. Added to this training was her keen sensibility to people. She had helped many appreciative clients. Some were students at the university, which was a block from her office. It was the time of student riots. Young people were disturbed; many had no sense of direction. The government was blamed, but the lack of direction which she encountered was from home environment. She worked hard with these grown-up children and they loved her.

Then her husband died. That, she thought, was the beginning. Her mother died soon after, and her daughter married, moved away, and never visited her. She was now totally alone, hurting too badly to return to counseling and too old to get other work. (Oh yes, age discrimination is still alive and well.) She was old. At fifty-five she was unwanted. How did this happen so fast?

Living off her capital for five years while waiting for the pittance she could depend on from Social Security, she felt trashed—thrown away—a beggar.

Society showed its disdain. Her friends had dropped her quite rapidly when her husband died. She was an embarrassment, an outcast. More and more, her sense of worthlessness weighed upon her, pressing her toward a depression which was foreign to her nature. One day she heard about Mensa. She decided to take the test and find out just how stupid she had become. If she had lost all her intelligence, dropping out of life might be the kinder thing to do for humanity. She took the test and not only passed it but was in the top percentile—at age sixty-nine.

Age does *not* diminish intelligence. This was her salvation. From that moment until now, it gave her confidence when others, far inferior intellectually, tried to rob her of it. Being neglected and alone became bearable with this knowledge. How many old people give up and accept society's verdict because they are too tired and beaten to fight? she wondered.

Why are we treated like this? Are we responsible? Did we raise monsters instead of children? These children are the ME generation, self-centered and selfish, and now they, too, are approaching old age. How will they feel when they are seventy-five? she wondered. Of course, they all believe it won't happen to them. After all, they have Ph.D.'s, M.D.'s, or J.D.'s. Nothing can touch them. By ignoring us, they can amass fortunes and all will be well. They sneer at us now—those for whom we voted education aid and whose privileges and comforts we fought and worked to obtain. They don't need us now and wish we would disappear. When their children copy their actions, what will they do, these poor characterless, cruel, selfish, soon-to-be-old people? I will probably live to be a hundred, and then I will know. Will I be able to bear it?

She remembered the rebuff she received a month ago at an art sale. Looking down her nose, the registrar had said, "We must show life, vigor, youth—the real nitty-gritty. What could you possibly know about life?" Her registration was refused.

After that episode, Nancy hired a young man to act as her agent. He was favorably received.

She must know how that sale went. This brought her back to the question she had asked her doctor. "Will I eventually be able to walk without crutches or a walker? Perhaps a cane?" Well, crutches or no crutches, her painting must go on. She wouldn't dare, however, to appear before any sales. If old ladies are bad, she knew, old ladies with crutches are worse.

She called the gallery and asked which painting had been awarded the blue ribbon, and if it was sold, for how much. The young lady who answered the phone said, "It was a beautiful painting by a young woman we haven't met yet. It's called *Thought*. It's so profound; so vibrant; so sad, and yet so hopeful. It sold for $3,000.00."

"The artist's name?"

"Oh yes, here it is. Nancy Longman."

"Thank you," said Nancy Longman into the phone.

Nancy smiled grimly as she replaced the receiver, leaned back in bed, and awaited her next onslaught. **Q**

So long as there are no readers to tell us what poetry is and what it isn't, people like Helen Vender or Ventner will tell us. So is it any wonder we're presented with the works of Amy Clampitt? Even if the book were to burst into flames on my desk, there'd be another just like it—because people like Venter/Vender would set them up again, and *The Atlantic* would publish them, and torpid drones would exclaim over their windy nothings, and so on and so on and so on. I guess the moral of the story is that there will always be bad poetry. People like Vennor must feel there is a great deal at stake with poetry, like academic appointments, something in the win/lose department, but certainly nothing like a voice from a life lived, or lost, or fought through. Friends came over for dinner and we were rereading Clampitt's poetry and trying to figure out what it was saying—if anything at all. Well, big breezy Greek things, let's sort of say. The poet Gazes Down from Her Heights and Distributes Elegant-Seeming comments Upon the World Sort Of. It says: I am not involved. It says: I am above it all. It says: I neither shit nor piss. It says: I am fastidious and clean. It says: I have never cheated, never lied, never been overcome. It says: *Nice* people are impermeable and airtight. Call it Floating Head Poetry. I remember one year seeing the Goodyear blimp nearly forced down over the old Potter house on the south ridge of the Lamine River Valley. A bunch of us kids were running across the fields because we thought the thing was really going to hit. But it was a most amazing thing. It didn't.

Jim is getting a lap-top. He is working on his Vietnam book. We went cross-country skiing yesterday—first time for Jim. I used to do it a lot. The snow wasn't too good, though—glassy and crystallized. I've been reading *The People's Guide to*

Mexico. Can't wait to get down there in the tropics and relax and be out of this Anglo-Saxon world of lawn architecture and high prices. We have been looking at a town called Jalapa. Up in the mountains, so the heat will not flatten us utterly. Been buying travel guides and asking people for advice. It's been so long since I was in a tropical place. This *People's Guide* even has instructions on how to build a *palapa*! You know, one of those palm-frond things wherein you lie airborne in Yucatecan *hamacas* and drink rum ten yards from the blue ocean. Jim's and my money will go much farther down there—and if I rent this house out, we'll be all set. I feel confident that Windy Greek Poetry is confined to New York, or at least the North Atlantic; but I tell you what—if I run into this stuff translated into good Mexican, *I* will burst into flames. **Q**

PATRICIA MARX *to Q*

Patty's NEW WORLD ORDER

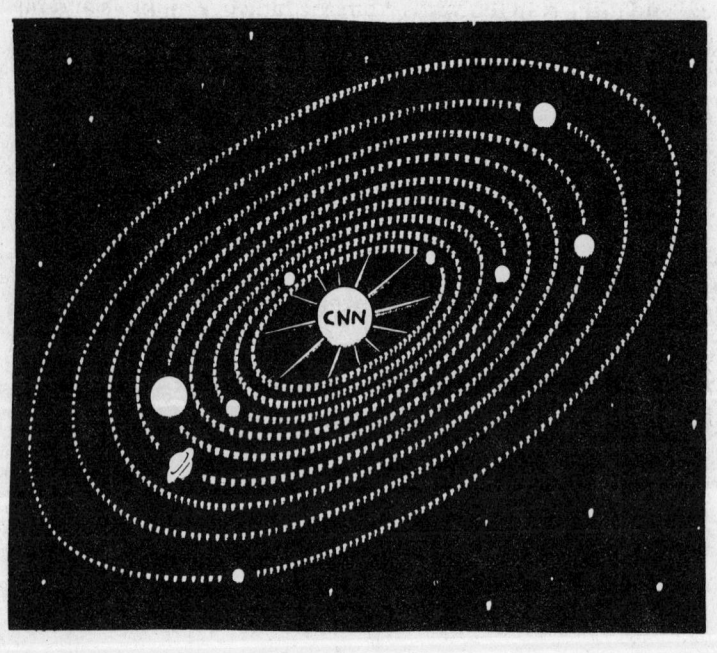

ENID CRACKEL *to* Q

Dear Mr. Lung;
God Bless you for "writing to me" in that letter that was on the front page, I never thot I would be famous, I'm just an Old Widow. What was that you said about being exposed in the same outlet as me? I could not understand that, being exposed, I am a Christian Lady you know. Are you saved, Mr. Lung? You have a friend in Jesus all the days of your life. I have seen those "pictures" that you draw in this magazine, I guess they are pretty, but some of them, My Goodness! One of those fellows looked like he could really use one of my Hawaian Rain Jobs! If you want to come here to the Home to visit me, can you bring a towel?

In His Holy Name,
(Mrs.) Enid J. Crackel, retired

ISABELLA BANNERMAN *to* Q

ISABELLA BANNERMAN *to* Q

THE LATEST TECHNIQUES FOR ABSORBING ESSENTIAL MINERALS.

ICE CREAM MERGERS

ANNA KAINEN *to Q*

What a lovely day, I thought on a Sunday afternoon in the park, as I watched elves dancing on the rainbow in the water fountain. Soon I became tired of concentrating on such innocent trivia, in which the human heart tries to find its own rhythm, only to drown in a sigh. I closed my eyes, and gradually I came back to the world in which my thoughts go bump in my mind. I returned to my usual way of thinking, and indulged in the occupation of people-watching.

If you're not interested in what I have to say, back up, man. Go some other place. Or if you believe in the generation gap, under thirty-something, or over eighty—STOP! don't read any further; you won't believe what you read anyhow, and there are so many more interesting things to do or read. Like what? Well, I'm afraid that there isn't much that I can teach you, but if you're five or six, your mother will gladly read to you, Hans Christian Andersen, "The Emperor's New Clothes," or *Cinderella*. Or else go to your teen brother or sister; they know more about sex, crime, or whatever the world is like out there.

If you're in your twenties, you had it all, and if you're eighty or so, what can I say that would make any difference, or any sense.

So let's start at the beginning, shall we? By the way, you may want to know what my age is. Ho-ho, that's one secret I wouldn't even trust my best friend with. Okay, so I'm not lucky enough to have a best friend, but for the sake of the records, shall we say I'm thirty-something?

But that's really irrelevant. I'm not here to disclose my age, my likes or dislikes, my waist measurement, or how I wiggle my butt in tight hot pants. The point of my story is— you are what you think you are.

Anyway, here I was on a bright sunny day in the park,

minding my own business. And what my business is—is watching the behavior of people, because, among other things, I'm also a lay psychologist studying the art of behavior, especially that of men.

Being an attractive woman, I often catch the eye of men looking me over. And believe it or not, even at my age I have something called a pounding libido when I see a guy I think I would like, and I wonder how he would be in bed. It's hard for me to imagine sex anywhere but in bed. This will tell you where I come from. You may ask, "What's wrong with sex in the hay or beach or wherever?" What can I say? I don't know. I never tried it anywhere but in a 6×4 bed with a soft mattress to sink into.

But let's forget the seamy side. Take it from me, the day I'm talking about was bright. Although it wasn't too bright for me. You know how it is, a woman without a man! But maybe you don't know. Maybe you have a husband, or whatever, who is "faithful." Pardon me, I almost choked on the word "faithful," which seems to be a real bone of contention getting stuck in my esophagus. Every time I hear a woman swearing that her husband is faithful, etc., I choke. Do you know why? Because through my own experience I know that the women who say that their husbands don't digress are either blind, and I don't mean blind where they can't see what the other women wears. No—they're blind where they can't see what their husband sees in the other woman.

Then there are the wise wives who say, "As long as he brings home the bagels and lox, and won't bother asking me every night, 'So, is tonight the night?' let him do his thing. I can deal with that. For them every night is the night. What pigs men are." The above is not my sentiment. I'm only quoting what I hear being said. Besides, I know the score, I was there once. But that's another story.

Now, let's not forget the wives who say, "What's good for the goose." Anyway, what with women's lib and other earth-shaking happenings, they allow themselves, without guilt, the pleasure of being free, and to bed down wherever with whomever happens to be at their disposal when the bedding-down desire strikes.

Of course, I don't blame them. I, too, believe in progress. If I had a husband I'd probably swap partners. A little change never hurts; it sort of makes things less dull and more exciting. Hell, why not? You know what I mean?

While I was pondering about this great *Weltschmerz*, I remembered an incident which happened to me not so long ago. I used to work in a place with a lot of Joes. They were all nice and impersonal. I'd ask them about their wives, their vacations, and they'd gush over their grandchildren. Who really cares?

One Joe named Leo—the boss—when he found out that I was divorced, I immediately became a person of interest. Not just a thing to push numbers.

One day, he came into my office to tell me how good I look. Next time, it was my new hairstyle he liked. Slowly he reached the point to say, "Hey, kid, I could go for you in a big way."

At first I didn't pay attention, but by the fourth or fifth time I said to myself, "There's something brewing in his kettle." Sure enough, his next move was on a bright sunny morning. "When are you going to have dinner with me, good-looking?" he asked.

"You name the day, Leo," I said.

"Will you really?" He beamed.

"Sure, why not—I'll save about twenty-five dollars and I won't have to eat alone," I said with a smile.

"Hey, that's great," he said. "We can sit and talk."

"Just give me a few days' notice," I said.

"Sure, sure. I'll find a way to get out of the house next week. Leave it to me, kid."

"It's not really that important, Leo," I said. "I wouldn't want to break up a happy family."

"No, no, don't worry, you won't. I just want to talk to you.

Nothing serious. I happen to like my wife. You understand. She is a good egg and we get along fine. It's just that you got under my skin. I think you are my kind of a gal. So, for sure we'll have dinner next week."

This went on for a few weeks—when he was free I was busy. Finally, one evening we were both free and we went out to have dinner as two friends.

His next move came a few days later. "Hey, kid," he whispered into my ear. "Can I come up tonight to see where and how you live?"

"No, Leo, forget it!" I pushed him away. "And I've been meaning to tell you that calling women kid, gal, or good egg went out with the sex revolution. Besides, at present I'm not in the marketplace. Especially not for married men."

"You mean if I were single it would be okay? That's a woman for you." He spit the words out.

I don't work there anymore. But when I'm like in a mellow mood, I can still smile at the foibles and games people play. Know what I mean? **Q**

JANE MARTIN *to* Q

Chapter 1
May 17, 1966

Now Everybody really Hates Me

Some people like me but it's rare. I ask lots of people to help me but they never help me much. My mother and father offen holer and scream at me. I am quite broke. I have around Six dollors and Very little cents (In money.) I have a room that I don't know if I'll ever get out of. If I don't, I won't have any food. and then I will die. which I want because nobody loves me.

Chapter 2
May 17, 1966

Now I will die

Just a few minutes ago I made my mind up. I will stay in my room for the rest of my life. unless we are having somthing good to eat tonight.

Chapter 3
May 17, 1966

BUT

But, if it's somthing bad, I will never come out again. If it's good it is will be my last meal.

Chapter 4
May 17, 1966

What About School?

When school comes I will go. But I won't kiss anybody in my family.

Chapter 5
May 17, 1966

What About Clothes

YING LING *to Q*

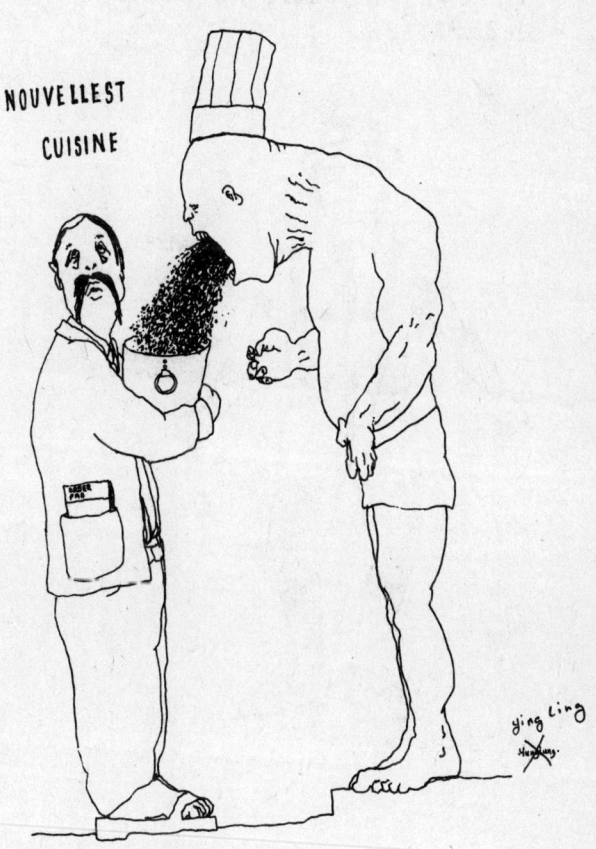

Nobody paid any attention to Friedrich until he put on lederhosen.

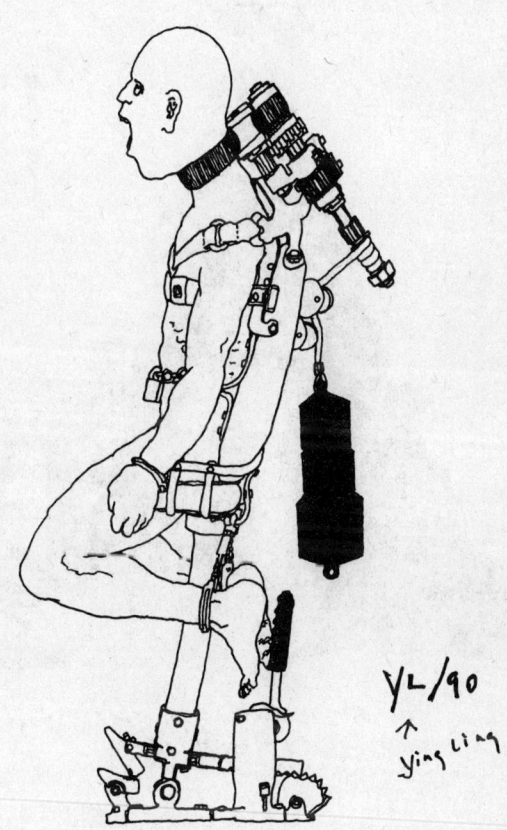

THE QUARTERLY

YING LING *to* Q

(This is supposed to be by Ying Ling)

We crossed the Rio Grande and arrived on the planet Mexico and drove as straightforwardly as we could. The sorghum crop was just coming in and we were caught up in convoys of trucks hauling mountains of sorghum seed. It was flat, dusty and full of things made out of sticks that smelled like gasoline. Spent the first night in a place called La Pesca, a hilly dry terrain of mesquite. There were elaborate hunting camps, like walled villas. We got a room in one of them.

The east coast gets mountainous south of Tampico. This is the oil-boom coast. It's crowded and dirty. You read in local papers about murders and robberies, and the pages are full of pictures of the shamefaced bandits with their stolen goods. These are called the "red pages," photos of the miserable captured unfortunates clutching blenders and tape recorders, typewriters, microwave ovens, and Cuisinarts, ragged fellows in huaraches. Spiky hair, bandages over their noses where the cops have knocked them with nightsticks. Went to Jalapa as planned. But it's a big town. About 600,000. Overwhelmed with traffic. Made a stab at looking for an apartment to rent, but the noise is unreal—buses without mufflers charging up narrow eighteenth-century streets. We were sort of cowering in the world's filthiest hotel. I'm talking dead roaches in the shower and piles of bird shit and a bird nest right in the room with you. So we chose this little town of Coatepec instead, which is smaller and is up in the mountains. It's a coffee town. They grow coffee here, and all around town are the beautiful tiled and barred mansions of the coffee barons; and a central park with araucaria trees and flocks of birds coming in every evening to roost, and church bells, and Xerox copy places. We found a splendid house, or courtyard, to rent. The house is about a hundred years old. What do I mean, about? It's right on a plaque on the wall in ornate gold and blue—June 10, 1894. Well, we are sort of camping out in one wing of the place. Where the other wing has gone to I don't know. I think it's down the street. The street, where this place is, is downhill—and so the rest of the mansion is lower than here, if this makes any sense. There are no ceilings; there are rafters holding up tiles twenty-two feet overhead, and termite shit drifts down in a light reddish rain. Jim says it's termite shit. He lies on his back, looking up, and says, "Jiles, that's *termite shit.*" There is a large terrace with stone columns, and arches, and a big pool with fish, and a lemon tree, and a chili-pepper tree, and palmetto, and hibiscus—that's over there in the middle. With tiles all around it. The windows to the street are ten feet high, with louvers and ornate bars. Beer is twenty-eight cents a bottle. We are suffering. War is hell.

Well, life in a Mexican mountain village is life in the streets, I am beginning to figure—you go to one place to buy tortillas, you go to another place for candles and batteries, another place for sacks of the local coffee. There's a funeral place that is open twenty-four hours a day. *Die Anytime!* It has inviting displays of coffins out in front. The streets are cobblestone or brick, and are lined with walls. Occasionally, you can see through a louvered window into a fabulous garden, through to a room with whitewashed walls where there will be a woman playing a piano. Down the street outside our door comes the milkman, or milk-child, pulling a large, reluctant buckskin horse, and the kid keeps stopping here every day, although raw milk has to be boiled and I'm not up to it, what with always having to dust the termite shit and keep writing. A loud-voiced woman comes by and browbeats me into buying hard cookies made of cornmeal and brick dust. They are the consistency of ship's biscuit, and okay, I buy some. Otherwise, the food is fantastic. I go to the market and am overcome by the fruit and vegetables. Then I come home to this mansion and hide out in a big white room and roll the paper in.

Mass went off this morning, at seven, with a great crashing of leaden bells. They don't have good bells at Nuestra Señora de la Luz. All the money went into gold work. But the women from this street are singing a novena for the soul of Anita Méndez, and every evening they sing the Rosary, and it's beautiful to hear. One of the mansions of the coffee barons has been made into the Casa de Cultura, and I went there in hopes of finding a place to work. There are photos all over the walls of the Maderistas, who were revolutionary soldiers, riding down the streets of Coatepec in 1920 or something, on horseback, with mustaches and bandoliers, and thin, hard noses, and then, hold your breath—the local poetess, yes, of 1921, posing delicately in a swing, with a high-necked blouse and a hibiscus over her ear. There is a monument to her in the alameda, the central park. In bronze. Xerox copies of her handwritten poems are framed on the walls of the House of Culture. Next to the hard-riding revolutionaries, in their grainy black-and-whites, the poetess is flowered, sincere. Her poetry emits rays of flowery light. She comments on the Latin poets of old. I go back to the Maderistas; I wish they had written something.

When we were coming down the coastal highway, it was a narrow two-lane, with no shoulders, which was all right in the flat, brushy mesquite country of the north, but when we got to the mountains of the Sierra Oriente, Jim had to do some driving. I mean some driving! There were eighteen-wheelers pulling out to pass us on ungraded curves, tearing around with no view of what was ahead, merrily slamming their air horns, great yellow tarps blowing wild off the cargo and about to come loose, vultures flying overhead in squadrons with great expectations. Then there were these things called *topes*—speed bumps—in the villages. There are rarely any warning signs that just ahead lies a speed bump as large as a dead body stretched out across the road (such as it is). What you might get is a tiny, tiny little sign written in skinny letters that says DANGER, TOPE. Anyway, in order to keep from taking off the oil pan and the entire undercarriage, Jim was always shifting to D$_2$ and standing on the brakes with both boots. Which caused our load—things like blenders, computers, the printer, the copy of *The Collected Works of Thomas Merton,* angle irons (*angle irons?* Jim insisted on bringing them, whatever they are)—to come leaning forward in a vast load-shift. And of course the *tope* is always right in front of the village restaurant, where your idlers and children are lounging about drinking Coca-Cola and waiting for somebody to bottom out on the speed bump. And so the little wretches shriek things like "Look out!!" etc. and go "Ya! Ya! Ya!" just like in a cartoon. What's worse is that some kids stand right on the *tope* because they know you have to come to a near-halt and creep over, so this puts them right at your window, and they can holler in at you, "Blue crabs! Delicious blue crabs! Money goes to the church!" Well, so do the corpses, I suppose, after they extract them from the wrecks. But there is no time to pause, as great cargo trucks with names like "Slicky Boy" and *"Espanta-Suegras"* ("Mother-in-Law Frightener") are boring down the highway not far behind you, and you must go onward, onward, ever onward, or get pretty powerfully bumpered from the rear. We saw a couple of *vaqueros,* of classic aspect, emerging from the bush with their great soup-plate Mexican saddle horns and hemp *reatas* and cocked hats—hard, smooth, beautiful Indian faces—and we wanted to stop and talk with them, talk horse, talk cow, but here comes *"El Dragon Negro"* with a load of concrete and there is no place to pull off the road except into a canyon. The meat store also sells baby clothes and plastic shoes, and the furniture store sells mangoes. Jim went off to a cantina the other night, and I feared they would bring him back slung across a horse (I saw a horse standing in front of that very cantina, and no kidding, it was tied up to its own foot). Or maybe they would have brought Jim back tied up to his own foot. But he came home happy. He goes to a bar called El Cototteos. I don't know what that means.

THE QUARTERLY

THIS SPACE IS RESERVED FOR JEFF BROWN.

(NOT FOR HIS WRITING BUT FOR HIM.)

PAULETTE JILES *to* Q

. . .

As for other social notes, we were invited to a rancho of some wealthy Mexicans near here. They had guitars and sang most of the night. They knew old sixties songs like "500 Miles" and "We Shall Overcome" and the one about the banks are made of marble, with a guard at every door. They expected us to know them; I knew most of them. It felt to me as if I were in a time warp. To hear these old protest songs from the sixties in this tropical jungle highland, in English with a heavy Spanish accent . . . it sank me. I had been running the streets in demonstrations at that time, and Jim had been in the Central Highlands getting mortared. Then we went up to a second-floor balcony for more rum, so we could watch the moon rise. It was full, and it made the part of the sky it was in entirely white, and it rose over the banana trees and the mango trees and the volcanic mountains. There was a terrific crashing sound in the trees that were right next to us, and I jumped away from the railing and over to the wall. I said, What was *that*? Frederico said, "Oh, those are the orchids. The plants grow very big and they get too heavy and they come down." It sounded to me like the size of a cabbage. Before long, another one, farther off, came down through the mango trees and the moonlight. Insecure, beautiful things falling down, the fall of the house of flowers. The next day, people started drinking at noon, a punch made of cow's milk and cane alcohol, so Jim and I took a couple of horses and went higher up into the mountains in the fog and wet and macadamias. Jim had a young black mare with an excitable mind. She couldn't keep all four legs going in the same direction at the same time—her legs were a perpetual source of surprise to her, as were the Zebu cows standing under the banana trees and the *campesinos* hacking at vines up on the slopes. But Jim is a fearless and skilled rider. It was hard for me to keep up with him. I had an old slat-sided gray. I beat on his butt with a stick. I never wanted to go back. I wanted to keep on. I figured we would find a lost temple, and inside the temple would be a secret passage, and the passage would lead to a weighted jade idol with an inscription, and the inscription would reveal the secret of being alive. But then our translation would be faulty, we would mistranslate a key suffix, and we would be left to work it out on foot. And so eventually we turned back. This time. The banks are made of marble, I tell you, with a guard at every door.

Well, I have a—ahem—*maid*. She comes to work in a dressy dress and high heels, and soaps everything. She washes the potted plants! She washed my underwear in Pepto-Bismol. She says she thought it was soap. Anyway, my brassiere looks like it's not getting any indigestion. **Q**

ROBIN CHMELAR *to* Q

I was wasting my usual time at the Quik-Stop perusing the *National Enquirer* and its like when I accidentally checked the T of C of *The New Yorker* (oops, almost forgot to cap that T) and found none other than the name Mark Richard. Top o' the roster, no less! What can this mean?

REPORTER AT LARGE	*Richard Blanchard*
A FRIEND WRITES	*Christine Schutt*
LETTER FROM WINNEMUCCA	*Sam Michel*
"FUCK YOU" (POEM)	*Stephen Hickoff*
"YOU TOO" (NOT A POEM)	*Rick Whitaker*
(NOT SURE WHAT THIS IS)	*Diane Williams*

COVER: *Nace*

DRAWING: *Yung Lung*

And, Jesus!

BOOKS, GOD, AND EVERYTHING ELSE .... *Gordon Lish*

Q

ENID CRACKEL *to* Q

Dear Rec. Director;
It was nice to hear that poet reciting her verse on Sun. afternoon, she is so talented, tho I did not understand every word, I could not hear sometimes. Is she famous? I met a famous poet once when I was younger, forget his name. Nice fellow, most poets are nice. The reason I could not hear was because I am 84 + my hearing is not so good anymore which upsets me you know, makes me feel older, but that old hag Mrs. Cronin had to keep her gums flapping the whole time. "What did she say?" she would scream out after every blessed line! How can a Lady hear what is being recited with that going on? I think you all should shoot that bitch full of some smack + give us Old Folks some peace!

Yours in Christ,
Enid J. Crackel, retired

Quality time

FOR CREDIT-CARD ORDERS OF BACK NUMBERS, CALL TOLL-FREE, AT 1-800-733-3000. PRICES AND ISBN CODES SHOWN BELOW. OR PURCHASE BY CHECK OR MONEY ORDER VIA LETTER TO SUBSCRIPTION OFFICE. NOTE ADDITION OF POSTAGE AND HANDLING CHARGE AT $1.50 THE COPY PER EACH COPY REQUESTED.

Q1	$6.95	394-74697-x	Q9	$7.95	679-72139-8
Q2	$5.95	394-74698-8	Q10	$7.95	679-72172-x
Q3	$5.95	394-75536-7	Q11	$7.95	679-72173-8
Q4	$5.95	394-75537-5	Q12	$7.95	679-72153-3
Q5	$6.95	394-75718-1	Q13	$8.95	679-72743-4
Q6	$6.95	394-75719-x	Q14	$8.95	679-72893-7
Q7	$6.95	394-75936-2	Q15	$9.95	679-73231-4
Q8	$6.95	394-75937-0	Q16	$9.95	679-73244-6
		Q17	$10.00	679-73494-5	